"Marry me, Melissa," Ran said

"What?" She stared at him, incredulous astonishment dilating her green eyes.

"I said—I want you to marry me."

Just for a moment there was a surge of utterly ridiculous joy, but then ice-cold reality returned.

"B-but you don't love me."

Ran laughed harshly. "Love, what's that? There's been precious little of that in my life. No, I'm afraid love's an emotion I've taken care to steer clear of."

The biting edge of his voice jolted her out of her daze as he went on. "That night when you walked away from me, I wanted to run after you, to shout you're mine, to beg you to stay. But you didn't. So when I saw you again, I made up my mind that this time I would have you."

Rachel Ford was born in Coventry, descended from a long line of Warwickshire farmers. She met her husband at Birmingham University, and he is now a principal lecturer in a polytechnic school. Rachel and her husband both taught school in the West Indies for several years after their marriage and have had fabulous holidays in Mexico, as well as unusual experiences in Venezuela and Ecuador during revolutions and coups! Their two daughters were born in England. After stints as a teacher and information guide, Rachel took up writing, which she really enjoys doing the most—first children's and girls' stories, and finally romance novels.

Books by Rachel Ford

HARLEQUIN ROMANCE
2913—CLOUDED PARADISE

HARLEQUIN PRESENTS
1160—A SHADOWED LOVE

BELOVED WITCH

Rachel Ford

Harlequin Books

TORONTO • NEW YORK • LONDON
AMSTERDAM • PARIS • SYDNEY • HAMBURG
STOCKHOLM • ATHENS • TOKYO • MILAN

Original hardcover edition published in 1989
by Mills & Boon Limited

ISBN 0-373-17069-6

Harlequin Romance first edition September 1990

CHAPTER ONE

'HEY, you there!'

The angry shout stopped them both dead in their tracks and, startled, they spun round. Now that he had attracted their attention, though, the horseman was seemingly in no hurry. As they watched, he trotted towards them down the wide woodland riding, sitting easily in the saddle, horse and rider a black outline against the low slanting rays of the early evening sun.

He was almost upon them when Melissa's green eyes widened with horror. She gave a tiny, strangled gasp of disbelief and stepped back hastily into the shadow cast by the tall overhanging sycamore hedge, at the same time shrinking further down into her aunt's oversized green waxed jacket and pulling the hood forward so that her face was lost in its capacious depths.

The rider, deliberately, she was sure, reined in only when the chestnut mare was almost thrusting against them. She felt a pair of hostile eyes survey her briefly from beneath the peaked riding hat, but then, almost before her hands had time to bunch themselves in panic, he had dismissed her as unworthy of notice and turned instead to her companion.

'I suppose you're aware that you are trespassing. This happens to be private land.'

His voice was colder, more authoritative than she remembered; a man's voice, not a boy's any longer—and a hard man at that. Beside her, she felt Jason bridle at his tone, and when she glanced quickly sideways at him she saw the flush of temper rise to his cheeks and his mouth tighten derisively as he took in the old brown leather jerkin and cord jeans.

'I don't think you quite realise who you're talking to.'

The man's thin lips curled ever so slightly. 'Why? Should I? Oh yes, how foolish of me,' he went on with transparently mocking humility, 'of course, you must be one of the bit actors who've been hanging around the village lately.'

Bit actor! From the scanty security of her hood, Melissa sucked in her breath in horror. Jason Hancox, handsome, charismatic star of half a dozen top TV serials and now filming the pilot for what would no doubt be a highly successful costume drama set in the once-turbulent Border lands between England and Wales! She'd known him only a few days, since filming had started, but could guess only too well how he would react to this calculated insult—and it *was* a calculated insult, she was quite certain. Despite all the years of separation, she knew instinctively that the newcomer was perfectly well aware of Jason's identity.

'Now look here,' the actor's ego was swelling almost visibly with affront and, too late, she put a warning hand on his arm, 'you ignorant bastard——'

Oh, no, not that! Melissa winced involuntarily and braced herself for the horseman to leap down and attack Jason bodily. She had once watched in horrified fascination as he half killed two boys who had hurled that same insult at him, then seen them limp away—no, one had been carried off covered in blood. But now, years on, he was, on the surface at least, more in control of himself, although fleetingly there was an expression in the storm-grey eyes which made her shiver.

'Right on both counts,' he said levelly. 'And if I catch you trespassing again down in these woods, you may discover just how much of a bastard I am.'

She saw Jason's hands clench themselves into fists. For his own sake, though, he must not be allowed to lose his temper any further—not with this man.

'No, Jason, don't!' Her voice, sharp with warning, disturbed the horse and it tossed its head, prancing sideways across the riding.

As Jason took a step forward, her hand tightened on his arm and, completely misunderstanding, he snapped, 'Look, rein your damned horse in, will you? Can't you see it's frightening her?'

He put his arm protectively round her shoulders, pulling her to him, but when she glanced up she saw that the rider was watching, not Jason, but her, leaning forward slightly in the saddle, his grey eyes narrowed slightly, as though to penetrate to the depths of her hood. She cursed inwardly. She should have stayed silent—something in her voice must have registered with him.

Abruptly she turned away, but she was too late. He neatly sidestepped his horse and before she could jerk back out of reach he had deftly twitched off the hood with his riding crop, sending her sooty black curls cascading to her shoulders.

'Well, well!' He raised one lazy eyebrow; he clearly was not going to allow himself such weakness as to show surprise. 'Melissa Grant!'

She wanted desperately to turn and flee, but from somewhere a long way down inside herself she summoned up all her reserves of pride.

'Hello, Ran, I didn't know you were back.' She was astonished at her own cool tone—for, after all, what on earth was he doing here in Stanton Morville? He must be working as bailiff—or gamekeeper perhaps—on the estate, now that the old family had gone from the Manor; he would certainly never have come before. Yes, that must be it. How ironic, though, that he should have come back, and be working here, of all places . . .

And yet, as she furtively surveyed him now through her sweep of black lashes, there was something about him that perplexed her—the way he bestrode the horse, the assured, even arrogant way he held himself—but then, she reminded herself, there always had been more than a touch of arrogance about him, even when there had been no reason at all for such pride. One thing she was absolutely sure about, though: whatever he was doing here, she would never have come within a million miles of the place if she'd known.

'Yes,' he replied, his cool tone more than matching hers, 'as you see, the prodigal son,' there was a slightly sardonic emphasis on the word, 'or perhaps I should say the black sheep of the village, has returned.'

She wanted to look away, but his wintry grey eyes

were inexorably holding hers. The sunlight, flickering and shifting through the trees, threw his face into stark shadow, and she felt a thread of unease, even fear, stir inside her. At that moment, as her reluctant gaze took in the hard, lean lines of his face—harder even than she remembered them—the dark, level brows, high cheekbones, aquiline, aristocratic nose, and the thin though beautifully moulded lips, he resembled nothing more than one of those cruel, predatory Norman Border barons whose blood coursed through his veins . . .

Jason, sensing the almost visible current leaping between them, cut in.

'Forgive me if I'm wrong, Melissa,' his beautifully modulated actor's voice was at its sweetest, 'but I gather that you know this—*gentleman*.'

'That's right, she does.' Ran glanced briefly at him, an all-encompassing, openly contemptuous glance, but before he could take up the sarcastic challenge in Jason's words Melissa said quickly,

'Er—yes. Jason, this is Ran—Ranulf Owen. We both grew up here in the village. I——'

'And so you must excuse us, but we have a great deal to catch up on, haven't we, Melissa?' Had they? Surely not. Surely there was nothing for either of them to say to each other, ever again? 'Such as, how is your dear father? Still as caring as ever for your welfare, I've no doubt.'

She flinched at the acid dripping from his voice. 'I——' she began, then broke off.

This wholly unexpected encounter—Ran, risen almost, as it were, from the ashes of the past—was knocking her completely off balance. For a few fleeting seconds she had naïvely allowed herself to hope that he, like her, had put the past safely behind him where it could do no harm, but it was inevitable, she realised with a plummeting heart, that he should still feel so bitter towards her father—and her. Despite the eight years that had passed, he had clearly forgotten nothing—none of the taunts, none of the pain, none of the betrayals . . .

'Dad's been very ill,' she said at last. 'He needs a milder climate, so he's given up his practice and they've retired to the Algarve.'

'Oh, I'm so sorry to hear that.' The mock solicitude did not fool her for an instant. 'But you'll excuse me if I don't weep too much for him. After all——'

'After all——' Anger was now stirring within her, blotting out the guilt, conscious as she was of Jason straining to pick up every titillating nuance of the scene unfolding before him. 'After all, you couldn't possibly understand that a loving father like him——'

She stopped, overwhelmed less by what she had just impetuously blurted out than by the sudden whitening of his tanned face. She bit her lip and whispered, 'Oh, Ran, I'm sorry——'

'Forget it, Melissa,' he said brusquely, then went on in a slightly more measured tone, 'What are you doing here? Are you acting in this film too?'

'Me? Good grief, no!' Melissa smiled at Jason, inviting him to share the joke, but he was scowling into the middle distance, so she went on, 'I'm working for the firm that's doing the catering while the company's here on location. They're using the old part of the Manor and some of the grounds for the filming.' She paused. 'But of course, if you're working on the estate, you'll know that.'

Ignoring the question in her voice, he merely nodded slightly as though assimilating her information, then, 'And your Aunt Olivia, how is she?'

There was a fractional softening of his harsh tone. Of course, her aunt had always had a tender corner of her rather tough heart for the boy Ran, and perhaps, invisible somewhere behind the adult Ran's impenetrable façade, there still lurked something of that unhappy, friendless child.

Relieved to be on marginally easier ground, she smiled slightly. 'Oh, she's fine. She's away at the moment on one of those plant-collecting expeditions of hers—in the Himalayas this time. I'm living in her cottage.' Ran's eyes flickered in Jason's direction and she added quickly, 'Jason's staying at the Morville Arms, although most of the cast are putting up at that new hotel near Shrewsbury.'

'Yes,' said Jason frostily, to neither of them in particular, 'I prefer to get well away from my fellow actors out of hours.'

'I can imagine that you might want to do that,' Ran responded, cordially enough, although there was no cordiality in his face or his eyes. He turned back to Melissa. 'I suppose you're on your way back to the cottage now?'

When she nodded, he went on, 'So that accounts for why you're trespassing in the private part of the estate. Correct me if I'm wrong, but I do seem to recall that the contract was for the use only of the grounds and woods to the west of the Manor.'

'Oh, I'm so sorry,' she snapped. 'But perhaps

you've forgotten that no one cared where the villagers went in the old days——'

'—The old days!' The savagery in his tone made her wince. 'Yes, you would remember them, wouldn't you, Melissa? But I'm afraid those days are gone—for ever.'

As though responding to the tension crackling in the air, the mare whinneyed and backed up against the opposite hedge, but Ran put a soothing hand on her neck. 'Perhaps you'll be good enough to bear that in mind in future.'

He favoured them both with a cold, not even marginally polite nod and, wheeling the mare round, jabbed his heels lightly into her flanks so that she broke away into a rapid canter, past a clump of silver birch trees and out of sight.

'Well!' Jason expelled a long, angry breath. 'What a charmer! Who the hell does he think he is, for heaven's sake?' When she did not respond, he added, 'And how come you know an oaf like that, Mellie?'

'It's a very long story,' she began reluctantly, but he broke in,

'And what on earth was biting him? I thought he was going to leap off that damned horse and flatten me!'

'Well,' she pulled a wry face, 'you didn't exactly put it very tactfully. You see, Ran is illegitimate.'

'So that was it!' He laughed, then drew her arm through his and they walked on. 'But surely no one cares about that sort of thing nowadays?'

'Ran does—or did,' Melissa murmured, as though to herself.

'I mean, these aren't the bad old days—you know, lecherous squire seduces innocent village maiden, and all that rubbish. Or *was* it something like that, Mellie? How romantic—and come to think of it, with those thunderous looks the guy's clearly a genuine one hundred per cent throwback to a mediaeval baron, or I'll eat my best doublet and hose.'

Quite involuntarily, there came into her mind an image of herself as a child. The whole Infants section of the village school had been messily engaged all term on a project on the Borderlands. The teacher had been given to powerful flights of imagination and the wide-eyed Mellie had seen the peaceful meadows and streams run red with blood, the English and Welsh dead piled high in every muddy farm gateway.

Miss Hughes hailed from the far side of the Border, from Wales, which evermore to Mellie would be that mysterious, legend-shrouded land which she could see from the top of the hill behind the village—and her sympathies had been all for the downtrodden Welsh. She was well launched one day on a fierce attack on the arrogant, invading Normans, describing in graphic terms their dark, saturnine features, when Mellie, struck by a sudden thought, piped up, 'You mean like Ran.'

The teacher had stopped dead and, encouraged by her silence, Mellie had gone on eagerly, 'You know, Ran—Ranulf Owen.' She'd jabbed a podgy finger at the helmeted knight in her book. 'He looks just like this.'

'Er—yes, Mellie. Now, children, if you'll all pay attention.' And Miss Hughes had gathered herself together to begin a vivid account of the Battle of Shrewsbury, which sat very queasily on top of school dinners.

Now, nearly twenty years on, Melissa could barely suppress a rueful smile. What an innocent! So cocooned in cotton wool by her parents, she must have been the very last person in the village to know.

'Know what?'

She was unaware that she had spoken aloud until Jason's voice chipped into her thoughts. 'Oh well.' She stopped, with a faint, dismissive shrug. She did not really want to discuss Ran with an outsider, especially an outsider as smooth and sophisticated as Jason. But what the hell? Ran had been his most unpleasant self a few moments earlier, as though taking a savage pleasure in humiliating her.

'He's the illegitimate son of Sir Ranulf——'

Jason whistled. 'Sir Ranulf! But doesn't his family own this place?'

'They did. He died a few months ago.' Melissa knew she should feel at least a token twinge of sorrow, but, unlike many of his ancestors, Sir Ranulf had done not one single thing of good for the estate and village, as far as she could remember.

'So who owns it now? Has he got any legit. heirs?'

'There's a son, but from what I've heard the death duties are so heavy that he's been negotiating to sell the whole estate.'

'And where does our charming friend on the horse come into the picture?'

'Well,' she frowned, 'Ran's six years older than me, so it must have been—oh, thirty years ago. It really is a bit like you were saying. His mother was a maid at the house.' She spoke slowly, with no taste for the story-telling, though after all, Ran's sordid history was common knowledge locally. 'Sir Ranulf denied that he was responsible, and her parents disowned her, but the old vicar took her in as his housekeeper. When Dad—he was the local doctor—delivered the baby, she said to him, he's to be called Ranulf, after his father.'

Melissa smiled faintly. 'That set the village tongues wagging even more, but the vicar insisted on christening him Ranulf, so there was nothing the family could do. And of course, as he grew up, there was no doubt in anyone's mind.'

'And what then?' Jason prompted her hesitation.

'Nothing, really. Sir Ranulf gave her nothing at all for the child, but when the vicar died he left her enough money to buy a cottage. She could have left the village then, but she was a proud, hard woman——' like her son, she thought, but did not say it '—and to leave might have looked like admitting defeat.'

When she stopped, Jason said impatiently, 'Well, go on,' but, catching the unpleasantly salacious gleam in his eye, she shook her head. 'He left the village over eight years ago and I haven't seen him since, until today. And that's all.'

All—except that I loved him. At sixteen I loved him so much that I thought, I really thought my heart would break when he went away. But Aunt Olivia said hearts were made of much tougher stuff than that, then dosed me up with some of her revolting herbal tonic—which didn't work, at least not for years and years.

Hardly aware now of Jason at her side, Melissa quickened her pace in a futile attempt to evade the painful images that were surging back . . . Her father had made no secret of his disquiet at the first hint of her teenage crush on Ran. A stern moralist of the old school, he had been appalled by the recurring scandals surrounding Ran's father's name, and as a family doctor he had seen at first hand too many instances of the sins of the father being recreated in the children. The casual fecklessness of Ran's legitimate half-brother—coupled with Ran's own wayward, at times downright anti-social behaviour—joined forces in his mind to produce an absolute antipathy towards him.

But the more he had tried to keep her away from Ran, the more seductive had seemed the aura of glamour around the tough young man, and she had haunted him like a fragile moth buffeting itself at a flame until its wings were burned away.

Many of the other village girls had fancied Ran, but there was always a hardness in him, a pride gone sour and driven in upon itself by his treatment at the hands of his father, which sometimes he had used deliberately, or so it seemed, to repel them. Only with the gentle Melissa—and then only rarely—had he relaxed, allowing her to glimpse the person he might have been—warm, teasing, rumpling her black curls and calling her his little green-eyed witch . . .

They were out of the woodland now, the track leading between tall hedges which were bursting into spring leaf, the ditches foaming with the acid-green of dog's mercury, right up to that old five-barred gate. Melissa stopped abruptly and turned away to lean against the gate, her chin on her hand, her face half averted.

'Nice view.'

From far away, she heard Jason's voice, felt his arm brush hers, but her stiff lips could frame no response. This was the gate where she had waited that other evening. It had been summer then, the night before she and her parents had been leaving for a camping holiday in France, and she really should have been at home, where her suitcase lay still almost empty on her bed.

At last she had seen Ran coming towards her up the field, his old working jacket slung carelessly from one slim shoulder. He had been avoiding her lately, she knew that—not unkindly, just melting away with a casual word or a smile whenever she appeared, which was worse than ignoring her.

Now, when he saw her, he hesitated as though to turn away, then came on, but more slowly. Often, he would vault the gate, even after a day's hard work, but this evening he stood the other side, silently surveying her, then opened the gate slowly, almost reluctantly.

'What have you got that ridiculous muck on your face for?' He had sounded angry.

Muck! Nina Green's mother's expensive French make-up!

'Nothing,' she said, a shade sullenly.

Ran rested his arm lightly on her shoulders. 'Sorry, Lissy. It's been a beast of a day. That calf I was hoping to save has died and the mother's in a bad way. Oh, damn!' He smacked his hand down on the gatepost.

She looked at him, seeing the lines of strain, the tension round his mouth, that had no right to be in such a young face. He worked all hours for any farmer who would give him casual labour, not so much for the money—though there was little enough of that—but more, she knew with that deep instinct which reached out to him, to deaden the pain and the hurt inside him. She put her hand up, to stroke away those harsh lines of strain, but he stood rigid under her soft caress, his eyes looking past her.

'Please don't be angry, Ran,' she said gently, and at that he seized her hand, burying his mouth in the warm palm, drawing her close to him with his free arm.

When her arms went round him in response, though, he broke her grip, thrusting her away from him almost savagely. 'No, Lissy.' Then, as she went to take his hand, 'No, don't touch me. Come on, I'm taking you home.'

He put his hand on her arm and began leading her, gaoler-wise, along the footpath, and when she risked a glance at him from under her lashes his face was grim and set. Black misery was washing about inside her—how could he be like this? She was going away for a whole month. Thirty days. How would she exist, dragging this memory of him around France? She closed her eyes momentarily and stumbled over a bramble, giving a muffled gasp of pain as it clawed at her ankle.

Ran stopped. 'All right?'

She nodded, shaking her hair forward at the same time to keep her face invisible, but he put his hand under her chin, turning her to him. His mouth twisted suddenly.

'Oh, Lissy, don't look like that! You must know how I feel about you. I love you.' When, dazed, she could only stare at him, he went on fiercely, 'But it's impossible. You're just a child still,' he managed a ragged smile, 'even with that muck on your face.'

Melissa shook her head vehemently. 'I'm not a child—I'm sixteen!'

He grimaced. 'There are sixteen-year-olds and sixteen-year-olds, Lissy.'

And what had happened next, the twenty-four-year-old Melissa thought suddenly, still resting her elbow on the gate, was pure Eve, taking on the shape of that innocent sixteen-year-old. Ran loved her—he wanted her. She put her arms around him, drawing him very slowly to her, and just as slowly she felt his tense body relax to her.

When she turned her face up to his, he muttered something quite incoherent and began smothering her face and throat with kisses which made her skin blaze with heat. One hand slid up inside her T-shirt, brushing across, then taking possession of the swell of ripening breast, so that she sagged against him with a little moan.

He put his arm around her waist and, almost lifting her off her feet, plunged away from the footpath to a magic place deep among the ferns and foxgloves. He undressed her with a fumbling tenderness that made her want to cry, before taking her in his arms and telling her over and over again, his mouth against her warm skin, that he loved her, that no one must ever come between them . . .

It was dusk when they roused, and now the magic

had gone. Ran looked withdrawn, almost as though
he was angry with her, and Melissa dressed quickly,
feeling the chill of separation already on her spirits.
They hardly spoke on the way back to the village, and
when they did their voices were stilted and unnatural
and they were constrained with each other in a way
they had never been before.

At the gate of her house she paused, thinking that
he would leave her there, but instead he slipped the
latch and, putting his finger to her lips, walked her
down the path towards the large, sprawling stone
cottage, one end of which was her father's surgery
and waiting-room. The window to the patio was
open and, hearing her parents' voices, she drew back
sharply into the shadow of a mock orange tree, its
white-wreathed branches catching in her hair. She'd
never been able to stand the scent of it, so sickly, so
overpowering, after that night.

Her father was saying something, his voice raised
in anger, then she heard her mother say soothingly,
'No, I'm sure she isn't, Roger.'

'Well, I won't have it, do you hear? Blood will
out—and there's plenty of bad blood in that young
man——' Dry-mouthed with terror suddenly at what
she knew was coming, Melissa moved restlessly, but
Ran's arm was round her, holding her relentlessly so
that she was forced to hear every word. 'Look at his
father—the morals of the farmyard—and it will come
out in him sooner or later. Mark my words, that boy's
heading straight for the devil. No,' stifling his wife's
murmured protests, 'if you think I'm going to allow
my only daughter to mix with——'

Beside her, Ran was standing as though turned to

stone, only his warm breath stirring the down on her cheeks, his hand closing on hers so that she almost cried out with the pain. When, terrified, she looked at him, his face was set in a contemptuous sneer, his eyes brilliant with barely-contained anger.

She heard '. . . wrong side of the blanket . . .' and winced with the same anguish which she knew Ran must be feeling. Somehow she had to stop her father. She moved against the bush so that the branches rustled, and a moment later he appeared in the doorway, peering out into the dusk.

'Is that you, Melissa?'

She gave Ran's arm a warning squeeze, then, breaking from his grasp, stepped out on to the path. 'Yes, Daddy, it's me.'

'Where've you been? Not been with that Owen lad, have you?'

She hesitated, the dark shadow which was Ran just behind her. Now was her chance to stand up for him, to shout from the rooftops, I love Ran, and he loves me, and there's nothing you or anyone can do about it!

'N-no, Daddy,' her voice was barely a whisper, 'of course I haven't.'

She went on down the path, setting her lips tight on the sharp twisting spasm of pain and guilt as she heard hurried footsteps, then the gate crashing to. Momentarily she stopped, before going on in to face the row over her lateness and the borrowed make-up, then to spend the next month being trailed listlessly around an endless succession of French caravan sites.

When they finally got home, Ran had gone. 'Been

left best part of a month,' one of the villagers told
her. 'Off working on a farm down Ludlow way, so I
hear.'

CHAPTER TWO

'PENNY for them?' Jason was regarding her quizzically, and Melissa wrenched her unhappy thoughts back to the present.

'Oh, they're not worth anything like a penny,' she said with forced lightness.

The sun had gone behind a cloud and the spring evening seemed suddenly to have turned chill. She shivered and, not waiting for Jason, began to walk on swiftly, almost as though to exorcise a shadow, a dark shape dogging her heels.

Aunt Olivia's small slate-roofed cottage was tucked away behind a holly hedge under the lee of the gently rolling hillside, while its owner, no doubt, was at this very moment striding purposefully among the jagged Himalayas, she thought with a smile.

As they went up the path, she cast an anxious eye over the shrubs and plants which filled every inch of the large garden. Well, they all looked fine—but of course the herbs which were her aunt's 'bread and butter' trade, to be sold to some of the local supermarkets and wholefood stores, were tough anyway. What she called her 'cream cake' trade—her rare climbers and plants, gathered during trips like the one she was on now and then propagated for sale to discerning gardeners—all those fortunately looked well too.

Melissa opened the front door and went to slip inside. ''Bye, Jason, see you tomorrow.'

But he put his hand on the door. 'Come on, Mellie, not again! Don't I get an invite in?'

'Oh, no, I'm sorry, Jason, but——'

'But nothing.' He was beginning to sound faintly exasperated. 'Your aunt's not back, so while the cat's away we can play——'

He put his arms round her, but she squirmed neatly out of them. She knew she ought to be flattered, but the very idea of 'playing' with Jason was somehow utterly repellent to her.

'No, I mean it.' She forced a teasing note into her voice. 'It's all right for you actors, swanning in and expecting your breakfasts to drop in front of you, but I've got to be there by five in the morning to cook for the make-up and wardrobe people.' She pulled a face. 'And you know we've got all those extras in tomorrow for the battle scene, so I really must get an early night.'

'All right, all right, point taken,' he snapped. 'See you tomorrow—if you can spare me a glance, that is.' And he strode off, swishing with his hand at a scented viburnum shrub growing beside the gate as he went.

Melissa sighed and went on in. She made a pot of coffee, carried it into the small sitting-room and switched on the gas fire, then slumped on the sofa, staring at the blue flames. Why hadn't she taken Jason up on his invitation—why indeed had she been keeping him, almost literally, at arm's length ever since the location work had started? He'd made it more than obvious that he was attracted to her, in spite of the blatant come-ons of half the women on the set, and he was certainly one of the most handsome men she'd ever met—far more handsome, in a conventional sense anyway, than Ran——

Oh, damn! Now why had she allowed that particular thought to sneak into her mind? She didn't want to think about Ran. She wouldn't let herself think about him, not for a moment longer. He'd made it perfectly clear what he thought of her; the contempt had crackled in his voice, his eyes. Her delicate face crumpled up for a moment in remembered pain. For him, no doubt, she now belonged among the ranks of the betrayers . . .

What *was* he doing back here—and on the estate, which all through his boyhood had been forbidden territory? If he really had come back here to work then it was as well, for both their sakes, that the location filming, at least for this pilot episode, was just about in the can. On the other hand, if it proved a success, as Chris, her boss, was confidently predicting, she would all too soon be back up here in Shropshire, and not just for a fortnight next time.

She cradled her coffee mug, gazing at the whirlpool of froth at its centre. Of course, she could always quit the job if that happened, but she didn't want to. She was really enjoying it, and besides, Chris had already several times hinted, in her bluff way, that there might soon be the possibility of a partnership. And surely, anyway, to throw up the job would be carrying things to extremes. It had all been such a long time ago, and in any case Ran, always a rolling stone so resolutely determined on gathering no moss, would probably disappear again soon as abruptly as he had that other time . . .

Melissa thrust all these disturbing thoughts from her. It really was true what she had told Jason—that what she needed, above everything, was a good night's sleep.

Melissa stretched out her legs luxuriously, made her back more comfortable against the rough bark of the old cedar tree and took a last bite of her salad roll, the only food she had been able to face for her lunch. Since five, she seemed to have been on an endless treadmill of preparing and serving, first breakfasts, then, by the time the final plate of bacon and eggs disappeared, moving straight into the first lunches.

Behind her, through the open windows of the enormous trailer, she could hear the clatter of pans and the excited chatter of the young students from the nearby catering college who had been recruited to cope with the influx of extras, including members of the Mediaeval Arms Society, who were taking part in the battle sequence that was to form the climax to the episode. Filming was in full swing again and from among the trees away to her left there came shouts and galloping hooves, punctuated by anguished squawks from a loud-hailer, as the fourteenth-century ambush was enacted for at least the third time.

Well, at least she could take a breather for half an hour or so, before starting on the teas that the battle-grimed knights and their camp-followers would no doubt be demanding soon enough.

'Hi, Mellie.'

Craig Fellows, one of the younger actors, was

standing over her. He peeled off the authentic-looking leather mailed jerkin with a grunt of relief and flopped rather disconsolately down beside her.

Melissa smiled at him. 'Hi, Craig. Finished for the day?'

'Well, I've done all my filming, but Marcus, the fights director, wants to go through my rescue scene again later, before we film it tomorrow.' He grimaced, his fair, boyish face clouding. 'We were supposed to get it done this morning, but I made a right cock-up of it. I nearly slit Suzie's throat, trying to cut her free and fending off friend Jason at the same time. It's really just getting the mechanics of the moves right—it's all been choreographed—but it just won't come. I really must be pretty thick!'

He slapped his forehead extravagantly, but she could see that underneath he really was bothered. A few days before, he had confided to her that this was his biggest role so far, and she had secretly suspected that he had been chosen for the part more on account of his magnificent physique—he was built like a young blond gorilla—than any outstanding acting ability.

She hesitated, then, with slight trepidation, said, 'Look, Craig, can I help at all? I don't mind taking Suzie's part for you to practise on—so long as you don't slit my throat, that is.'

His face lit up. 'Would you really, Mellie? Oh, that's great! Come on.' And before she had time to repent of her rashness, he had dragged her to her feet and was striding off, with her in tow.

Beyond the catering and filming paraphernalia there was a winding, overgrown thicket and beyond that again a small lake, hardly larger than a pool.

'You should really be strung up to the Market Cross as a witch,' Craig remarked, as he tied her swiftly to the trunk of a willow tree at the water's edge, the cords cutting uncomfortably through the thin voile of her white blouse and her short pale blue drill skirt, 'but this'll have to do. Right, now I have my sword in this hand, my dagger in the other, and . . .'

. . .'Got it!' Craig, at long last, shouted in triumph, and Melissa, who had spent a traumatic half-hour in terror for every delicate part of her anatomy, opened her eyes to see him grinning down at her. He threw down his weapons and she straightened up, flexing her fingers and toes painfully.

'Mellie darling, you're a honey!' He swept her up exuberantly into his arms, her feet dangling off the ground, her slim body pressed to his, and planted a smacking kiss full on her lips. 'Thanks a million. Now I must go—Marcus'll be waiting. Won't he have a surprise!' He set her down, gave her another bear-like hug, and raced off.

Melissa was just gathering her shaken wits together when she became aware of a man, leaning against a tree a little further along the lake, arms folded, watching her. As he slowly uncoiled himself and began to walk purposefully towards her, she turned and took half a dozen swift steps in the opposite direction, but then she heard him call peremptorily, 'Melissa!' She slowed and reluctantly turned back as he came up to her.

'I-I can't stop, Ran,' she said. 'They'll be wanting me for the teas.'

His face was grim and after one swift glance she found she was unable to quite look at him, focusing instead on one of the buttons of his blue short-sleeved casual shirt.

'The teas can wait. I want to talk to you.'

He put his hand on her arm, drawing her back into the seclusion of the trees. His touch was lighter than Craig's, and yet his warm palm against her bare flesh was sending little prickles of electricity up her arm in a way which Craig's grip had totally lacked. He loosened his hold and leaned casually against a silvery beech trunk, surveying her. Now that he had detained her, she thought resentfully, he was in no apparent hurry for the talk which had been so important. She stared at the grass, littered with the husks of last year's beechnuts, uncomfortably aware of his eyes roving over her.

At last he spoke. 'That was an interesting little scene.'

'Oh, I was just helping Craig. He's been having problems with one of his fights.'

'He didn't seem to me to be having any problems.'

'Well, he was. We must have got it right by the time you arrived,' she replied, her nettled tone an instinctive reaction to the coolly sardonic inflection in his voice.

'Every time I see you, Melissa, some man is draping himself all over you. Tell me,' Ran swept over her gasp of outrage, 'are you bent on working your way through every half-way presentable man on the set by the time——'

'How dare you!' Melissa, her face scarlet, raised her hand. If the blow had fallen, it would have been a

stinging slap, enough to force him back on his heels,
but with whiplash speed his own hand seized her
wrist, bending it backwards until tears of pain sprang
unwillingly to her eyes.

'L-let me go, will you!' she panted furiously,
writhing in his grip, but his hold only tightened.

'Say please.' His voice was a soft taunt in her ear.

'No, I won't, damn you! You're nothing but a
bullying—ouch!' His fingers tightened even more,
until her skin almost burned under the pain, as he
wrenched her even closer to him.

She jerked her head back, but could not escape the
expression on his face. How hard he looked, she
thought, with a flicker of real fear, the lines of his
thin, high-boned face unyielding, the latent cruelty in
his thin lips far more pronounced than eight years
before. Her throat tightened in panic—here was a
man, she felt sure, who would take a savage delight
in hurting, even destroying, anyone who wronged
him in the slightest way.

They stared into each other's eyes from a distance
of six inches, she outwardly defiant, he—she could
not quite read the expression in his grey eyes, but
suddenly his lips twisted and he relaxed his hold,
pushing her away from him.

'I'd forgotten just how stubborn you are. I suppose
you'd still be refusing if I screwed your arm right off.'

'That's right.' She glowered up at him through her
tangled black curls, nursing her wrist tenderly, where
the marks of his fingers were already puffing up in a
purpling semi-circle.

'I'd also forgotten just how bewitching those long
green cat's eyes can be.' He was regarding her now

with a disturbingly ambivalent expression in his own eyes. 'Is that how you're doing it, Melissa? Casting a spell on all those poor fools of actors?'

My little green-eyed witch . . . Even as his teasing words of long ago leapt unbidden to her mind, she saw him run his hand through his thick dark hair. In the old days it had been longer, shaggy even, but even so something in the familiar gesture rocked her suddenly to the very core of her being.

How handsome he was, and how inevitable it had been, that teenage infatuation. It really was just as well that her heart had painfully mended, though perhaps the shattered pieces had not quite come together right. Since Ran, Melissa had never been able to summon up more than a passing interest in any of the young men she had met—which made his accusations now all the more unjust. Disconcerting tears were pricking hotly behind her lids, and to cover up her uncertainty she glared at him.

'Oh, do me a favour, will you? Go and jump in the lake. I've told you, I was only helping Craig. He's—well, he's just like a gorgeous overgrown Labrador puppy. Quite harmless—unlike some people,' she added belligerently.

Ran laughed, though without amusement. 'Hmm. Maybe, though that young man doesn't look much like a Labrador puppy to me. But it's the other one—Jason Hancox. He is not gorgeous, that one, not at all.'

Her jaw dropped. 'I don't believe it! Are you warning me off Jason?'

He nodded sombrely. 'Yes, I am, Melissa.'

'Well, of all the——'

'I've met his type too many times lately, and I don't like them.'

'Oh, really? And I'm supposed to take note of your opinion, am I?'

'In this, yes, you are,' he said sternly. 'I'm just warning you—don't play around with Hancox. You don't seem to have heard about his reputation, but underneath all that glossy charm, which you've obviously fallen for, he's essentially weak, and like a lot of weak characters he can turn very nasty.'

'You seem to know a lot about him,' she snapped.

'Yes, well, he's got quite a reputation in some quarters. Some friends of mine in the City have put money into a couple of movies he's been in, and——'

'The City?'

'Yes.' He raised his dark brows in mock enquiry. 'Why so surprised, Melissa dear? Have I still got hayseeds growing behind my ears, or should I perhaps be wearing a smock and gaiters?'

'N-no,' she stammered, 'of course not, but I didn't know you'd——'

'And talking of clothes, maybe it's not witchcraft, after all, that you're using on these guys.'

There was a new undercurrent in his voice and her eyes narrowed. 'And what exactly do you mean by that?'

With cool, almost insolent deliberation, he allowed his eyes to travel slowly over her body. 'Well, far be it from me to criticise your wardrobe, of course, but do you have to be quite so provocatively free with your charms?'

Melissa stared first at him in stunned incomprehension, then, as a swift flush of pink deepened in her cheeks, down at herself. It was true, of course. Her skirt *was* very short and the voile of her sleeveless blouse very fine, clearly revealing the white lacy bra and the high swell of her breasts. None the less——

'It may come as news to you,' she said icily, 'but provocation couldn't be further from my mind.' And when he gazed at her in frank disbelief, she went on, 'This happens to be my working gear—under an overall, of course. Maybe you've never had to prepare and serve up to fifty cooked meals at a time in a cramped trailer, but you need to be sensibly dressed, I can assure you. And speaking of work, that's exactly what some of us should be doing now, so I must go—that is, of course, if you'll *please* excuse me.'

And with that, she swung on her heel and stalked off across the grass back towards the catering area.

Chris, not looking at all pleased, was standing at the foot of the big trailer steps, and Mellie groaned aloud. Those fruit scones for the company's afternoon break should have been in the oven by now. What a way to try to seal a partnership! She waved and began to run.

It was early evening before they left the site, Mellie for her aunt's cottage, to nurse a thumping headache brought on less by the stress of the day's work, she told herself angrily, than by that encounter with Ran, and Chris for the pleasant country hotel where she was staying.

Mellie had offered her Aunt Olivia's pretty spare bedroom, but her boss had refused, though not so much, she was sure, from any delicacy of being beholden to her employee as to give herself a free hand with Denis, the producer, with whom she had seemed to be getting very close, and Mellie had told herself that if that was her way of ensuring they got the contract for the follow-up series, well, that was her business.

Now she pedalled down the quiet village street, but then, as she turned the corner, she jammed on her bicycle brakes so violently that she almost shot over the handlebars. She balanced on her toes, frowning in perplexity at the cars parked by her aunt's gate, one a battered Cortina saloon, the other a sleek Jaguar, its grey shark's nose thrusting across the verge.

She leaned her bike against the holly hedge and walked slowly up the path. As she went round to the side kitchen door, she heard an unfamiliar man's voice and—— Hurriedly, she pushed open the door.

'Aunt Livy, what on earth are you doing back? Are you all right?' Her aunt, normally so hale and weatherbeaten, was sitting at the kitchen table, looking very pale and drawn, while a tall, elderly man was bending over her.

'Hello, Mellie.' She managed a weak smile for her niece. 'Sorry to surprise you, but I—I wasn't too well, so Arnold here very kindly——'

'Oh, phooey,' the man broke in gruffly. 'No kindness. Had enough walking—only too glad of the excuse to find us seats on the first flight out. Your aunt's picked up a nasty bug, my dear. Nothing serious, but the party doctor thought it as well to get her home, call in her own doctor, and all that.'

He broke off, looking expectantly at Mellie, and she pressed her fingers to her throbbing temples, trying ineffectually to summon her scattered wits for action. 'Oh, yes, of course——' she began hesitantly.

'So if you'll just stop gaping like a stranded goldfish——' A new voice, all too horribly familiar this time, chipped smartly in, and her head swivelled to the corner of the kitchen, her mouth sagging open. Ran had been screened by the door as she had flung it open, and was obviously enjoying every moment of her discomfiture. Now he straightened up. '——we'll get her to bed.'

She allowed herself just one swift, hostile glance, then said frigidly, 'There's no need for you to be here. We can manage quite well, thank you.'

But Arnold was picking up his woolly gloves and scarf. 'Well, I'll be getting on my way, then, Olivia, now I've seen you safe into these two young people's hands. Long drive down to Cornwall.'

'I'll see you off,' said Mellie. Perhaps by the time she returned Ran would have had the grace to accept that he wasn't wanted and remove himself.

In the gateway, Arnold hesitated. 'Ring up in a couple of days, if I may. See how she is.'

'Yes, please do, and thank you for everything.' Mellie smiled warmly at him, then began leading the way to the Jag, but he laughed.

'No, this old banger's mine,' he patted the aged Cortina's roof affectionately, 'though I maybe wouldn't say no if that young man of yours were to offer me that beauty in exchange.'

He nodded towards the other car as, too dumbfounded even to react to 'that young man of yours', she closed his car door. Ran with a sleek new, horribly expensive Jaguar? Was she imagining it, or was the world in the process of turning upside down? She waved Arnold out of sight and slowly retraced her steps.

She found them upstairs, her aunt leaning back on her bed while Ran unlaced her sturdy shoes. When she appeared, hovering in the doorway, he stood up. 'You help her undress, while I go and ring Dr Morgan.'

'I've told you, I can manage perfectly well,' Mellie said between her teeth, pitching her voice very low. 'There's absolutely no need for you to stay.'

But he merely said, with cool deliberation, 'And then you'd like a cup of tea, I'm sure, Olivia.'

Oh, tell him to get lost, Aunt Livy, *please*, Melissa willed with silent desperation, but her aunt smiled up at him. 'I'd love one, thank you, Ran.' So Melissa could only accept his fleeting glance—not exactly of triumph but certainly of inward satisfaction—and tighten her lips on the spasm of thwarted anger.

As she gently but quickly helped the older woman undress, her mind was busy. What was he doing here? Why wouldn't he go? Why had he insisted on staying? Merely to annoy her, no doubt—and equally clearly to try to disturb her. Well, she had to admit that he'd succeeded on both counts. His calm commandeering of the situation had angered her, but worse than that, she could feel something deep inside her—she wasn't sure what—insidiously untwining itself and could see her fingers trembling slightly as she helped her aunt on with her nightdress and into bed.

'Thank you, Mellie, love.' Olivia smiled wanly up at her. 'Sorry to be such a bother. I'll be all right in a day or so, I'm sure. And how are you—how's this job of yours going?'

'Oh, fine, Aunty, thanks. Chris seems quite pleased with me——' apart from this afternoon, that is, she thought ruefully, '—and she's even been dropping hints about a partnership, which would be really great.'

She heard a slight noise behind her and turned to see Ran in the doorway, holding a tray of tea.

'Dr Morgan will be here in half an hour.'

He bent to set down the tray on the bedside table and Olivia patted his cheek. 'You're a good lad, Ran.'

'Nonsense. It was just lucky that I was passing when you arrived.'

As Melissa watched, he caught her aunt's hand and pressed his lips to it, then, as if to obviate the need for further speech, he straightened up and said briskly, without a glance in her direction, 'I'll be off, then.'

'Yes, you go along. I know you're busy.' Her aunt smiled again. 'And Ran,' he paused in the doorway, 'I'm so glad, so happy for you.'

''Bye, Olivia, take care.'

He gave Melissa a cool nod and then, as she stared unseeing at the closed door, she heard him clattering down the stairs, no doubt having to duck his head under the low beam into the kitchen, and moments later, just below the window, a car engine throbbed into powerful life.

Rousing herself, she poured a cup of tea and handed it to her aunt, and then, as she poured herself one, asked casually, 'Er—what did you mean, about

Ran—I mean, being so glad, so happy for him?'

'Oh, hasn't he told you? He said he'd seen you.'

A faint, chill finger of unease touched her mind. 'No. Told me what?'

'Ah, well,' her aunt looked irritatingly mysterious, 'if he hasn't said anything, I don't think I ought to. But I'm sure you'll find out soon enough . . .'

Much later that evening, with her aunt sleeping soundly upstairs, Melissa was half dozing in front of the television, and sipping a mug of hot milky drink . . . Dr Morgan, her father's former partner, had arrived as promised and had diagnosed a rather unpleasant virus.

'She'll be all right, but I've no doubt she'll be quite low for a few weeks. Perhaps it's as well that you'll be here during the nights.'

'Oh, but,' Mellie had felt a sharp stab of guilt as she spoke, 'I'm due to leave in a couple of days. Our next assignment's up in Yorkshire and I'm sure they won't be able to do without me—not at such short notice.'

'Now, don't you worry, my dear. We'll manage perfectly well—there's an excellent nursing agency that I'll get in touch with.'

Mellie knew that Olivia would be angry with her if she stayed, but none the less she was still feeling slight pangs of self-reproach. To try to shake them off, she allowed her mind to stray back, reluctantly, to those words of her aunt. *So glad, so happy . . .*

But surely, when did people ever say that, except—she was wholly unprepared for the pain which shot through her like one of Craig's sword-thrusts, brutal and savage—except when someone was getting married? So that was it. Ran was getting married!

CHAPTER THREE

'FOR heaven's sake, girls, haven't you finished yet? We should have been packed away hours ago!'

Oh, no! Melissa's heart sank. Chris was obviously in one of her foulest moods. She'd seen her and Denis locked in what looked like a heated argument at lunchtime, and she clearly hadn't yet got over the row, or lovers' quarrel, or whatever it had been.

'Mellie, can I have a word with you, please?'

Taking off her overall, Mellie shook her hair free of the white cap. Giving the subdued-looking students a commiserating smile, she followed her boss out of the trailer, her pulses doing a rapid pit-a-pat. Apart from the trouble with Denis, this last day had gone really well. Even more extras had been drafted in for the final battle scenes, but they'd coped—and she knew, with a glow of inner satisfaction, that she'd more than played her part in keeping on top of the potential chaos.

So maybe this was the moment. Perhaps this, in fact, was why Chris was so much on edge. There would no doubt be problems to a working partnership with her. She was a tough businesswoman and given to fits of temper out of a clear blue sky, but they soon passed, and there was no doubt that she was highly efficient—and very ambitious—so the firm looked set for success. When

Mellie had rung her father to tell him of the
possibility, he'd said he'd be delighted to buy her
into the business. 'About time you settled down into
a steady job, at the ripe old age of twenty-four,' he'd
teased . . .

'Er—Mellie,' Chris began hesitantly, her voice
unusually constrained, 'I know this'll come as a bit of
a shock for you, but I'm—well, that is, my plans have
changed, and I'm not going to be able to keep you
on.'

Melissa stared disbelievingly at her, the ground
lurching beneath her feet. 'You mean—you're giving
me the sack?'

Chris pulled a face. 'I prefer to say that I'm
terminating your employment.'

'But—but why? Look, if you're not ready for a
partnership yet, don't worry. I——'

'*No*. I mean, it isn't that. I'll give you a marvellous
reference, Mellie. You'll have absolutely no problem
getting another job. In fact, a friend of mine in
London is planning to take someone on. It's similar
sort of work—you'd love it, I'm sure.'

'But I don't understand——'

'Well, these things happen.' Chris wasn't meeting
her eyes. 'You know how it is in our trade.'

Melissa frowned slightly. There was something
funny going on here. She could sense it—*smell* it,
almost. Chris was not at all her usual self—blunt,
frank to the point of rudeness. She was looking
thoroughly evasive—even shifty. Suddenly, the
scene she had witnessed between her and the
producer flashed into her mind.

'Denis—has he got anything to do with this?'

'Denis! Good grief, no. Why should he?'

But the vehement denial rang hollow. Just what had she done—what could she possibly have done to upset Denis to this extent? After all, they had had virtually nothing to do with each other. Unless . . . Could he possibly have decided that she'd been unprofessional in some way, perhaps through being over-friendly with the male actors—just as Ran had implied? Ran! Had his delaying her yesterday and making her late meant that she'd blotted her copybook so badly that Chris had decided that she needed someone more reliable? In that case, this was all Ran's fault. But surely not—that was far too trivial. There must be some far more potent reason than that for Chris's abrupt decision.

She yearned to ask, to beg her to reconsider, but pride kept her silent.

'Not to worry, Chris. I understand perfectly,' she said at last, in as steady a voice as she could manage.

Her boss—her *ex*-boss—looked highly relieved, glad no doubt that she wasn't going to make a scene, start hurling threats about wrongful dismissal. She handed her a fat envelope.

'Er—there's a bit extra there, Mellie. Buy yourself a nice present.'

Mellie wanted to tell her to keep it, but, determined on making a dignified exit, she only said stiltedly, 'Thank you very much.'

'And you'll come to the end-of-shoot party tonight?'

Melissa hesitated. She longed desperately to rush off now, this instant, pour out her disappointment to Aunt Livy, then hide herself away in her bedroom, but once more pride stiffened her backbone, like a whalebone corset. Almost imperceptibly, she tilted her chin and drew her slim body up an extra inch.

'Yes—yes, of course I'll be there.'

'Oh, good.' The relief was palpable now. 'You get off now, Mellie, and see how your aunt is. We can finish here.'

As she cycled slowly back to the cottage, Mellie grappled with the effort of coming to terms with this abrupt turnaround. Well, she thought ruefully, so much for being indispensable! Just one consolation in the whole miserable business—at least now she had the chance to stay on here for a while and help look after Aunt Livy, to repay her just a fraction for all her kindnesses over the years. She certainly couldn't afford to stay out of work for long, though, and she knew well enough that there was precious little chance of her finding a suitable job locally.

When she got back, her aunt was awake, and Melissa told her vaguely about having left her job, but fortunately Livy was too drowsy to ask any awkward questions. Once alone in her bedroom, though, her determinedly cheerful expression dimmed. In spite of her brave words to Chris, for two pins she wouldn't go tonight. She'd ring up Livy's friend and tell her there was no need, after all, for her to come round and 'aunty-sit'.

Everyone would know by now what had happened, and could she really bear the pitying looks, or worse, the quiet innuendoes? Perhaps they all—and not only Denis—thought she'd been too familiar with Jason and the others, like him, mistaking her natural open friendliness for something less innocent. On the other hand, if she didn't turn up, they'd put her down as a chicken-hearted coward as well. She clicked her tongue in indecision, then, as the grandmother clock downstairs chimed seven, she got to her feet and went off to shower and wash her hair.

Most of her better clothes were in her flat on the outskirts of Birmingham, and so, back in the bedroom, she hesitantly trailed her hand along the wardrobe rail. But surely she needn't worry too much? From what she'd seen of the cast, they seemed to spend their free time—perhaps as a reaction to their elaborate mediaeval 'working' costumes—in clothes so casual as to verge on the scruffy.

Finally she pulled out a blouse in pale pink ribbed cotton, a touch of the Edwardian about its high, lace-edged collar and puffy, elbow-length sleeves, and a pale dove-grey skirt, also in heavy ribbed cotton. Mmm—oldish, but they'd do fine. At least Ran wouldn't be able to indulge in any taunts this time—she was firmly enclosed from chin to mid-calf in opaque cotton. Not that it mattered what he thought—and anyway, surely he wouldn't be there. Just as well, though—he would no doubt have found some caustic remark about her bare arms—— Oh, for goodness' sake, *stop it*! she said fiercely to herself, don't even think about him.

Her mirror reflection frowned back at her. Her ivory skin was paler than usual. Well, she spent so much time in a hot, mobile kitchen these days. It *was* only that, and not the residue of shock over her dismissal, she told herself stoutly, as she set about remedying the ghostly pallor with blusher, a vivid pink lip-gloss on her generously wide mouth, mascara and a light dusting of the gold eye-shadow which always intensified the green of her eyes to a soft feline brilliance.

She brushed through her mop of dark curls, then gathered a handful of hair into a knot at the back of her head, leaving the rest to fall to her shoulders. Hearing a gentle knock at the front door, she wriggled her feet into flat white pumps, and tore downstairs.

The big pink and white striped marquee had been erected that afternoon on the sweeping lawns, and as Mellie walked up the drive she could see it almost pulsating with music, laughter and talk. Lights glowed through the canvas, throwing into stark relief against the evening sky the big house behind it. There were just two or three lights on inside the Manor; the rest of it was in sombre darkness, only the faint moonlight touching the far end, the original thirteenth-century section, and illuminating the castellated battlements and deeply recessed stone windowsills, as though sprinkling them with hoar-frost.

Somewhere in the shadows around the enormous front door, she knew, was that small shape, carved in the stone and familiar to her since childhood. Casual visitors had always taken it to be a lucky horseshoe, but the locals knew better. For them, it was a slender sickle moon, emblem of Hecate and symbol of witchcraft. The old legend said that it was placed there by a beautiful girl. She'd been brought before one of the first Border knights to live here, accused of witchcraft. He fell madly in love with her, and married her.

Whatever the truth of it, centuries of weather and reaching fingers had blunted that mysterious stone. Just for a second Melissa hesitated, feeling the hairs on the back of her neck tingle with the old excitement, her fingers itching to trace again its curve, as she had so often done as a child. Then she walked quickly away across the grass to the marquee.

She hovered rather hesitantly in the entrance, her eyes sweeping rapidly over the mêlée, then widening in horror. Oh, no! She ground her teeth in chagrin. So he was here after all, across the far side of the tent, wearing a pale blue cord jacket and trousers and navy polo sweater-shirt. Glass in hand, he was talking animatedly to Denis—so, like everyone else, he must know. But what on earth was he doing here? Keeping an eye on the place for his new boss, presumably, making sure the riff-raff didn't step out of line.

Her lips tightened involuntarily at the memory of their last abrasive meeting, then, a split-second before she sensed those grey eyes moving to focus on her, she ducked behind some hefty props hands who had just arrived in a boisterous group. Under cover of their broad shoulders she sneaked over to where some of the young catering students were sitting and dropped into a seat beside them, well screened from Ran's penetrating gaze.

Someone thrust a drink into her hand and imperceptibly she began to relax, so much so that a second drink even gave her the courage to venture out of her hiding-place and dance when Craig asked her. The music ended, but before she could sit down again Jason, in a cream shirt and tight black trousers, appeared at her elbow. His face was flushed and his blue eyes were sparkling with good humour.

'Hi, Mellie. You look delicious.' He made a mock growl. 'Good enough to eat!' He put his arm round her waist and drew her firmly to the edge of the crowd. 'Heavens, it's hot in here! Let's go outside.'

She hesitated. He had obviously been drinking, but he seemed quite sober still, so she allowed herself to be drawn out into the night.

'Now what's this I hear about you and Chris splitting up?'

'Oh, well,' she said lamely, 'I decided, with my aunt being ill, and one thing and another——'

'That's not what I heard.'

So they did all know. 'I—I'd really rather not talk about it, Jason.'

'Of course not,' he said comfortingly. 'It's a damned shame, though. Poor little Mellie!'

He pulled her closer to him and, preoccupied with her own thoughts, she did not resist. They had wandered down a narrow walk, bordered on one side by a huge overgrown hedge, and she stopped dead suddenly.

'Oh, the maze!' she exclaimed. 'I'd forgotten all about it.'

She darted ahead, pushing aside the overhanging branches. 'Yes, here's the entrance. There's a story that it was built in one night by a witch——'

'Never mind that!' Jason caught hold of her roughly and when she saw the expression on his face her stomach somersaulted with fear.

He was blocking her way out, but she forced herself

to babble on. 'She's supposed to have——'

'Oh, shut up about the bloody witch. What about us?'

'Us?' she repeated stupidly. 'Whatever do you mean?'

'This.'

The surprise of his swift action, dragging her into his arms and kissing her savagely, made her for a moment helpless, but then she wrenched her mouth away, nauseated by the smell of stale whisky.

'Please—let me go!'

She was panting for breath, the very real fear drying up her voice to a croak, but he only laughed.

'Not this time, my darling. You've been playing hard to get quite long enough.'

'Jason, please, you must——'

'Let you go? Oh, no—at least, not until——'

One hand seized her blouse front, wrenching the buttons apart, then, sickeningly, she felt it close on her bare breast, the sweaty fingers paddling urgently in the soft flesh. She opened her mouth to cry out, but he smothered the desperate plea with his own lips, his teeth biting cruelly into the tender skin.

Dizzy, almost fainting with terror, she closed her eyes, then, dimly, she heard him give a grunt of pain and his hold on her was loosened suddenly. When her eyes opened she saw that Ran, his dark face suffused with fury, had got hold of Jason by one arm and was swinging him round, as though he were a rag doll, his clenched fist already raised for the blow.

'No, Ran, don't!' Mellie was shaking with fear, not for herself now but for Jason—and for what Ran, his face murderous, would do to him.

But he brushed her off so that she reeled back against the hedge and landed a volley of swift punches on Jason's face and body. As the actor stood swaying helplessly under the onslaught, Ran gave him a vicious knee-kick in the groin.

'Now, get out, you filthy little tomcat!' he spat out at him. 'And if you ever lay a finger on her again, I'll kill you with my bare hands!'

Jason, bent almost double, gave them both one fleeting look of baffled rage, and stumbled out through the gap in the hedge.

More than anything, Mellie longed for Ran to take her into his arms, to shelter and comfort her, but one look at his face told her that it was far more likely that, having demolished Jason, he would now start on her. Her whole body was shaking so much that her legs would barely support her, yet some instinct for self-preservation shrieked at her that she must get away. But almost before she could move towards the entrance he had cut off her escape route.

'Are you all right?' Despite the question, there seemed to be no concern in his voice, only an icy contempt.

She hugged herself, her fingers clutching convulsively on the sleeves of her blouse as she tried to still the trembling in her body which was like an ague. 'Y-yes.'

It was all she could force out through her chattering teeth. The shock, both of Jason's assault, then his violent removal, was making her lightheaded, but she struggled desperately to pull herself together.

'It—it wasn't half as bad as it looked, Ran.' Terrified by the anger she sensed still blazing within him, and now directed against her, she fought to make the lie convincing. 'He'd been drinking, and I could perfectly well have——'

'Don't be a damned fool! If I hadn't seen you sneaking off, guessed what was in that evil little rat's mind, and followed you, you'd have been in real trouble. Raped—yes, *raped*,' Ran repeated savagely as, feeling the nausea churn in her again, she turned her head away with a faint whimper of protest, 'and you know it.'

He expelled a deep breath and through the claustrophobic darkness she saw him run a hand through his hair.

'Just what the hell did you think you were doing, Melissa? Are you absolutely crazy? *No*——' as she ineffectually tried to stoke up enough anger to protest '—I saw you leading him into the maze.'

She hung her head, miserably aware of how the scene must indeed have looked. Totally useless, she knew, to try to explain that it had only been her innocent interest in the long-forgotten maze!

'The poor fool,' he gave a harsh laugh, 'he might almost have been forgiven for thinking that you were as hot for it as he was.' Ignoring her gasp of outrage, he swept on fiercely, 'After all, it wouldn't be the first time you've led a man on, would it?'

When she was silent, he seized her by the shoulders and shook her. 'Would it?'

In the midst of her terror, Mellie felt momentarily the old anguish spurting inside her like bile. Of course, that must be how Ran saw her, how he always thought of her. A tease, a selfish, heartless little seductress, who could walk away from his love with a 'No, Daddy, of course I haven't been with Ran.'

'But it wasn't like that, not at all,' she said dully.

'Oh, really?' The contemptuous irony chilled her into silence, making stillborn the protestations she desperately longed to make: that she really had loved him, but that at sixteen the other pressures on her had quite simply been too great for her to withstand.

'These men that I regularly find you entwined with—did you really think that there would never be any comeback?' He paused. 'But maybe that's precisely what you did want——'

'No!' The taunt had at long last pricked her into angry self-defence. 'And just mind your own business, will you? You're not my keeper, you know—I'm a big girl now.'

'Yes, I can see that. Perhaps you'd like to cover yourself up.'

When she glanced down, she registered for the first time that her blouse was hanging off her shoulders, her ivory breasts gleaming pearly-pale in the moonlight. She gave a shaky little gasp and, hastily pulling up the blouse, began fastening it. But several of the tiny buttons had been wrenched off and her fingers were trembling so much that she was fumbling quite ineffectually with the others.

With an impatient exclamation, Ran pushed her fingers aside and swiftly did up all the remaining buttons, right to the two on her throat. His touch was light, even briskly impersonal, but deep inside her, his skin brushing against hers was making her shiver in a totally different way.

'Thank you,' she whispered, moving back from him.

They regarded each other in silence for a few moments, his grey eyes opaque, unfathomable, then all at once she began to quiver again, even more violent tremors running through her.

'I-I'm cold,' she said, though that wasn't the reason, and she knew that he must know it too.

But he only said, 'Of course—it's chilly out here.' Shrugging off his cord jacket, he draped it round her shoulders and immediately she felt the warmth from his body enveloping her.

Once they were outside the maze, riotous party sounds drifted to them, but when Ran turned in that direction she shrank back. 'I—I'm sorry, but I can't face going in there again.'

'I'll run you home, then.'

'No—please. You go back. I'll be all right now, but I don't want to go home yet.'

Her voice was still strained, and he put his arm lightly round her waist. 'Come on.'

He steered her across the lawns, to where the grounds sloped gently upwards to the woodlands. There was a ramshackle-looking rustic seat which Ran tested gingerly before pushing her gently down on to it, then sitting down beside her, his long legs sprawled out in front of him. Very conscious now of his nearness, Mellie edged away slightly, to leave two or three inches of bare wood between them, but when she glanced at him from under her lashes he did not seem to have noticed her furtive movement.

Drained perhaps by the turmoil of his physical and verbal outburst, he seemed now to be plunged into some deep private introspection, and they sat for some minutes without speaking. At first she was grateful for this, for it enabled her gradually to subdue her tumultuous feelings, but after a while his silence became unnerving and she risked another sideways glance at him.

His face was in shadow, the moon obscured by a fast-moving cloud. Seeing him like this, his familiarity lost in a blurred outline, she sensed only the vitality, the sheer animal vigour of the man. In that instant, a ripple of fear, far stronger even than the terror she had felt with Jason, ran through her. She was afraid of this faceless stranger beside her, of the power—no, the threat emanating from him. Her throat felt constricted, but she forced herself to speak.

'It's really overgrown, the maze, isn't it?' Her voice, even to her own ears, sounded stilted, but when he did not respond, she went on tentatively, 'In fact, the whole estate seems very run-down.'

'Yes, it is. Look at it.' His voice was grim and his gesture swept across the grounds. 'Those trees over there, still lying where they fell in last winter's gales, the brickwork of the Orangery crumbling to shale, the roof of the keep needs releading. A beautiful place like this—it's criminal!'

There was a throb of vibrant emotion in his voice, so at odds with his customary cold demeanour, which startled her. 'But surely, after everything——' no, this was too dangerous ground '—I mean——' she floundered to a halt, and Ran picked up her words.

'You mean, why the hell should I care if the whole place falls down in five years?' He gave her a wry smile. 'Surprisingly enough, I do. It makes me very angry. My father—it's all right, Melissa,' as she gave a nervous start, 'didn't deserve the good fortune to be born to all this. His total lack of responsibility to——' he hesitated fractionally'—all those he had a duty towards was just one small part of it.

'It's only now becoming apparent that, drunk or sober, he was utterly uncaring of the estate as well. Not content with turfing out any of the old tenants when it suited him, he seems to have got into the habit quite early on of selling off family treasures whenever he was short of cash. His——' again he hesitated for a second '—son is obviously cast in the same mould. Rather than struggle to keep the place intact any longer, he hasn't been able to get rid of it fast enough.'

'So it really is sold. Poor old house,' Mellie said sadly. Then, 'And you're working for the new owners?'

'You could say that.' Ran's tone was wholly noncommittal.

'What exactly——?'

'How's Olivia today?'

'Not too good, I'm afraid. But at least I'll be staying on here for a while now—just until she's on her feet again, that is.' She broke off, then went on, 'You've no doubt heard—everyone seems to have done—I've lost my job.'

'Yes, I did just hear something to that effect.' His voice was bland. 'Will you be looking for another job round here?'

'Oh, good heavens, no.' She laughed ruefully. 'I'll probably have to move to London. Chris——'

'This work of yours—have you got any qualifications?'

'Well, after my catering diploma I did an advanced

course in hotel and institutional management—you know, restaurant control, personnel administration, that sort of thing. I was working in a hotel in Birmingham when the job with Chris came along.'

'Hmm. And I suppose now you wish it hadn't.'

'Well, I thought it was going quite well. I was certainly enjoying it, until——' Her voice tailed off miserably.

'Of course, you could always come and work here.'

'Here?' she echoed, looking round in astonishment, as though half expecting a job to pop up, like Excalibur, from the middle of the lake which she could just make out beyond the trees.

'Yes. In fact, you could be the answer to a prayer.'

'But doing what?'

Ran gave her a sudden, wholly disarming grin, his teeth white against the dark shadows of his face. 'Setting up and running the catering side of things for us.' And when she stared at him, 'We're establishing a conference centre here, based at the Manor. Nothing too large—sixteen to twenty delegates at a time. As well as all the usual facilities—syndicate rooms, audio-visual equipment, learning walls, etcetera—we aim to provide everything a bloated businessman's overstressed little heart could desire. A swimming pool, health leisure area, and nine-hole golf course.' He grimaced. 'I've just been waiting for this wretched filming to finish—I only agreed to it as a favour to Denis—and the landscape designers will be in.'

He paused. 'Of course, the guests will expect first-class restaurant facilities while they're here. We've already got a chef lined up, but we need someone to oversee it—and it looks as if we've just found her.'

Melissa's mind was reeling. It was a wonderful opportunity, of course, the chance to use the skills which had remained virtually unused since college . . . And besides, there was Aunt Livy . . . But on the other hand, she would presumably be working side by side with Ran . . .

She temporised. 'I—I don't know. I'm not very experienced.'

'Oh, I believe in giving youth its head,' he said gravely, though she was almost positive that laughter danced privately behind the gravity.

'But your boss—won't he want to interview me himself, or at least give me the once-over?'

'Melissa,' he was laughing quite openly at her now, 'I'm my own boss—I'm the new owner of the Manor.' And then, as she gaped at him in utter stupefaction, 'Maybe I should have told you earlier.'

'Yes, you should,' she snapped. Sheer panic was setting in; he simply mustn't be! It was hard enough for her to cope with her vision of Ran as he had been, without having to upgrade him a few thousand notches.

'What did you do for money?' she blurted out, but then, slightly ashamed of her rudeness, 'I'm sorry, it's just——'

'It's just that you remember me without a penny to my name. No better than a common labourer—that was your father's phrase, wasn't it?' She winced at the raw bitterness. 'And I'm sorry to disappoint you. I know you much prefer me as a penniless nobody—you no doubt consider me easier to handle that way——' Easy to handle? That wasn't in the least how she would have chosen to describe Ran, either now or in the past.

'Eight years is a long time, Melissa, particularly when someone is as hungry, thirsty for success as I was.' He turned and looked full at her. 'I've never told anyone this before, but when I was about ten I sneaked into the Manor grounds one Midsummer Eve, into the maze. Yes,' he smiled, though without a trace of amusement, at her gasp of shock. No one, certainly no child, ever went into the maze alone—and above all, not on that night of all others.

'I went to the very centre. I'd brought a dead fieldmouse I'd found.' He smiled wryly. 'You have to take a present for the witch—remember?' Melissa nodded slowly. 'I made a pact with her—offered her everything, including myself, if she would give me this house.'

'And what happened?' The old childish fear was trickling like cold water through her bones.

He laughed. 'Well, the wind rustled through the hedge, an owl hooted, I dropped the mouse and didn't stop running till I reached the village!'

'But it's worked,' she said wonderingly. 'The spell, I mean.'

Ran nodded sombrely. 'It worked.'

He paused for a moment, then, 'When I left the village——' in the darkness, Mellie tensed but his voice was quite detached '—I went to work on a farm near Ludlow. The owner wasn't a real farmer—he was something big in the City—and pretty shady too, sailing very close to the wind of actual criminality. That's when I first had my eyes opened as to just how much money there is swilling around for anyone who

wants it badly enough. He was away most of the time
and Ginny, his wife, was—lonely. She seemed glad
of someone to talk to—especially pillow-talk.'

He glanced at her, but she willed herself to stare
straight ahead, forcing from her mind all visions of
Ran and this unknown Ginny in bed together.

'She was a little tramp, of course, but I more than
kept my side of the bargain.'

At the casualness of his tone, Mellie swung round
now, to see his profile outlined against the sky. The
hard ruthlessness that she saw in it put goose-
pimples on her arms. That woman—he had used her
sexual desire for him coldly, heartlessly, she had no
doubt, to extract secrets from her which she had no
right to give.

As though to confirm her thoughts, Ran went on
reminiscently, 'He was furious when he found out
what she'd told me—and even more when he
discovered that I'd used the information, plus the
money from my mother's cottage when she died, to
make a quick killing. And that's how I made my first
million!'

He took her hand, holding it lightly between his,
though when she tensed, his fingers tightened just
enough to warn her not to struggle.

'So why not give in gracefully? I'll make you an
offer you can't refuse—double the salary you got
from Chris, and think of all the experience you'll get.'

Mellie did not reply at once. Could she really
handle a situation where, inevitably, she would be
working in such close proximity with him? She'd
been vulnerable enough to the old Ran. Wouldn't she
be walking into the very heart of the fiery furnace if

she were to come here to work for him? A hundred
times more handsome, more polished, more lethally
attractive . . . Something very like terror was swirling
through her mind, so that she wanted to leap up and
run away.

And yet, whatever her feelings for him, he had
made it more than clear that any tenderness he might
once have felt for her had long since died. The
bitterness at what he so clearly saw as her betrayal
was still there, though, simmering a hair's breadth
beneath the surface. And yet he was so obviously
determined to make a success of this new venture
that surely he would not be willing to jeopardise it in
order to gain some sort of private vengeance on her?
In any case, she remembered suddenly, though with
a fleeting, treacherous pang, Ran was getting
married, wasn't he? So she really did have nothing to
fear.

'Yes, all right, Ran, I'll take the job, if you really
think I can do it satisfactorily, that is.'

'Oh, I'm sure you'll be more than satisfactory.'

He stood up, his face a pale blur, but she sensed
triumph behind the evenly spoken words. He pulled
her to her feet.

'I'll get the car and take you home.'

Ran drew up outside the cottage and flicked on the
interior light, then, with a sudden exclamation, he
put his hand under her chin and turned her face
closer to him.

'Your lip's bleeding.'

Melissa put her finger up and for the first time felt
the stickiness of drying blood on her swollen mouth.

'That swine Hancox!' His lips tightened and before she could protest he had taken out his handkerchief and was dabbing gently at her mouth, his touch butterfly-soft. Their faces were very close, and when their eyes met there was something intangible yet infinitely disturbing in his expression which made her gaze slide past him in confusion, her breathing suddenly rapid and uneven.

'Th-thank you, it's fine now.'

Conscious that her colour had risen, she turned away. She was still fumbling with the catch when Ran leaned across, his arm brushing her body, and opened the door, but then he held it firmly to, so that she could not escape.

'I'll see you tomorrow morning, then,' she said, in her best businesswoman's voice but still without looking at him.

He released his hold and she almost fell sideways off the seat in her anxiety to be safely out of the car. As she went to close the door, though, a sudden thought hit her.

'Is that what Aunt Livy meant?'

'What?'

'When she said she was so happy for you. That you'd bought the Manor?'

'Yes, I'd just told her when you arrived. Why, Mellie? What did you think she meant?'

And before she could frame a reply, Ran gave a soft chuckle, pulled the door to and accelerated away into the night.

CHAPTER FOUR

'I'M so sorry.' Melissa, laden with parcels, had backed into the woman as she emerged from the doorway of the kitchen suppliers. Then, as she turned round, the woman exclaimed,

'Good heavens—Mellie!'

'Chris! How nice to see you.'

Together they edged back from the busy pavement, crowded with late afternoon shoppers and commuters trying to get ahead of the Birmingham rush-hour.

'And to see you, Mellie. But what on earth are you doing here? Buying up half the shop, by the look of it!'

Now that the initial surprise was over, Melissa could sense the constraint behind Chris's words, so she smiled warmly.

'You could say that. It's to do with my new job. I'm helping to set up a new conference centre that's about to get off the ground.'

'Are you now?' Chris's eyes did a lightning inspection of the expensively casual Indian cotton suit in indigo and pale navy checks, which Mellie had treated herself to on the strength of the contents of her first salary envelope. 'Well, that's great. I—I'm so glad things seem to be working out OK.' The embarrassment was there again for a moment and she hurried on, 'You certainly look as if you're thriving on it.'

'Oh, yes, I'm really enjoying it.'

And yes, Mellie thought, enjoying it she certainly was. The last few weeks had been frenziedly hectic but also intensely satisfying. As soon as the film crew had left, an army of overalled ants had descended on the Manor, swarming all over the house and the estate. She herself had been engaged in lengthy talks with interior designers, planning the dining area and supervising the installation of new equipment in the huge but hopelessly antiquated kitchen. She had reluctantly agreed to the removal of the enormous old Aga stove, but had at least rescued the few good quality copper and steel utensils from a century's accumulation of dirty pots and pans.

She had seen very little of Ran. He was away for days at a time, and whenever some instinct told her that he was nearby, he was perfectly correct, with just enough of the impersonal employer about him for her to be able to settle with relief into the role of dutiful employee. Although he wasn't exactly free with his praise, she sensed that he was happy enough with her work so far, and she, for her part, was revelling in the feeling of being a vital, and valued, part of the new enterprise. Just occasionally she would catch him watching her, a veiled expression in his grey eyes which made her slightly uncomfortable, but then she would shake off the feeling of vague unease with yet another stint of hard work.

'And how's your aunt?' asked Chris.

'Oh, she's much better, thanks. In fact she's away

at the moment, convalescing down in Cornwall, but I'm still living at her cottage.'

'You are? Where are you working, then?'

'At the Manor.'

'The Manor?'

'Yes. You remember it was for sale? Well, it's been bought by Ran Owen. He's the one who's turning it into——'

'*Ran*? You're working for Ran Owen?' Chris's eyes were almost bulging with astonishment—and something else.

'Yes. When you—when my job folded, he asked me to take over the——'

'The swine! The cunning swine!' Chris's face had flushed red with outraged anger.

'W-what do you mean?'

Mellie suddenly felt as though she were teetering on the edge of an abyss, which she could not see but could sense, opening at her very feet, and she could almost feel her toes curling inside her shoes, as if to draw back from the precipice.

'What do I mean? Are you telling me you don't know?' Chris eyed Mellie narrowly, then gave a hard laugh. 'Obviously not, my poor innocent. Just this—it was Ranulf Owen who was responsible for me dismissing you.'

She wasn't hearing right—she couldn't be.

'But——' something very peculiar seemed to have happened to her voice '—but it was Denis, wasn't it?' She looked almost pleadingly at Chris.

'Well, Denis was the one who leaned on me, but that bloody Owen was leaning even harder on him. No dismissal—no use of the Manor for any future series—simple as that.' Chris gave a bitter laugh. 'I thought he must have got a down on you from way back, but if he's——'

She broke off, shooting Mellie a speculative look which made her writhe inwardly, but somehow she pulled herself together.

'I—I really must go, Chris. Been great seeing you. Goodbye.'

Almost before she had turned away, though, her stiff smile had faded. Somehow, without being quite conscious of what she was doing, she found her way back to where she had parked Aunt Olivia's car, loaded her parcels and began negotiating the busy streams of traffic.

As she mechanically braked and accelerated, one thought only was shrieking in her mind. It was Ran. He'd done it—he'd been the cause of her dismissal. What had Chris called him—cunning? And so he was—a cunning, devious devil. But more than that—he was utterly ruthless. Just as he'd used Ginny, so had he traded on his hold over Denis, completely cold-bloodedly, to get at her. But how could he have done this to her—and why? Chris's words came back to her . . . 'got a down on you from way back' . . .

But then she heard again Ran's smooth words when she'd told him of her sacking . . . 'Yes, I did just hear something to that effect'. . . and her unease was obliterated by a gush of white-hot anger. Just you wait, Ranulf Owen, she hugged her fury to her, I'll kill you! I swear I'll kill you for this . . .

* * *

The front door of the Manor was opened by Mrs Pearson, the stout, elderly woman who acted as Ran's housekeeper.

'Why, you're back, then, Mellie.' One of the many villagers who had known Melissa since pram days, she had no time for any formal nonsense about Miss Grant.

'Mr Owen,' Mellie was tight-lipped, 'is he in?'

'He is,' Mrs Pearson said doubtfully, but then, as Mellie stepped smartly into the hall, she added, 'but he gave strict orders that he wasn't to be disturbed.'

'Don't worry, Mrs Pearson.' She gave the housekeeper a reassuring smile. 'I won't disturb him.' Just kill him. 'Where is he?'

'Well, he's through in the new exercise area. He's been out all afternoon, and he did say——' The housekeeper was almost panting in her effort to keep up with Mellie.

'Look, you needn't come any further. He won't even know I've seen you. He'll think I've slipped in the side door.'

Ignoring the woman's feeble protest, Melissa strode off in the direction of the leisure area. The double doors were locked and she stood for a moment, toying with the idea of kicking them in, then she remembered the fire exit door at the rear of the building. She opened it and slipped quietly inside.

The exercise studio and gym were deserted. The pine sauna was empty too, although there was a back-and-forth trail of damp footprints leading between it and the showers opposite. Thwarted temporarily, she stood tapping her foot, then, hearing a faint noise, spun round. Of course, behind that trellis screen was the whirlpool bath, only installed a couple of days ago. He must be in there.

He *was* in there. Mellie pushed the beaded curtain aside and stood, unobserved, in the arched doorway. Ran was lying back in the large circular bath, his eyes closed, a half-empty glass of whisky comfortably within reach. Huh, she thought bitterly, perfectly at his ease, as though he's never done a twisting, underhand thing in the whole of his life!

But now that she was here, what was she to do? Screech at him, Get out of there, so that I can knock you back in? She stood irresolute, impotently aware of her angry resolve paling rapidly into feeble irresolution. Damn him—even here, not even conscious of her presence, he was somehow in complete command of the situation.

Well, she'd change all that. Her eyes roamed feverishly round. Perhaps she'd make a start by smashing that rubber plant over his head? Then, in a small alcove, she saw a neatly-coiled white hosepipe attached to a tap on the wall—presumably to wash down the tiled area around the pool.

Her furtive footsteps were drowned in the rush of bubbling blue water. She picked up the end of the hose, put a trembling hand on the tap and risked another swift look at Ran. Such a pity—he looked so comfortable, so utterly at peace with the world . . . She carefully aimed the hose, lining him in her gunsights, then turned the tap full on.

As the jet of icy water hit him full in the face, he

uttered a sharp obscenity, then threw up his arms to protect himself, sending his whisky glass skewing across the wet tiles.

'Turn that bloody thing off,' he roared, 'or I'll——!'

His voice was choked by the gush of water, but there was no mistaking the malevolent fury and just for a moment Mellie wavered, half regretting her rash action. If he climbed out, she would be trapped in her alcove, the only way of escape a narrow tiled ledge leading back to the sauna area.

'No, I won't!'

She aimed another powerful burst at him, then, as he made a lunge towards her, she threw down the hose with a yelp of terror. As she turned to flee, her foot caught in the pipe and she fell headlong on top of him, completely submerging him and knocking the breath out of her own body.

Her one thought now was to get away. Spluttering for air, she put both hands on the side of the bath and one foot on the ledge, but before she could haul herself out she was seized from behind and dragged back.

'What the hell are you playing at?'

His voice shook with rage and, even as she still scrabbled ineffectually at the smooth edge, her heart quailed. What a fool she'd been! She should have gone home to cool off, as all her common sense had told her, and then confronted him in a controlled, dignified way. But now all that she had done was unleash a thunderbolt, which was about to descend on her head.

'Come here, you!'

Behind her, she felt him put his arm round her waist and give her a sharp tug, breaking her frantic grip so suddenly that they both fell back in a heap again. This time Ran was the first to recover. He seized her roughly by the shoulders and pulled her down on to her knees in the middle of the jacuzzi, where the powerful jets played against their legs so that they swayed slightly to keep balance.

Her hair was plastered all over her face in seaweed-like strands, but when she pushed it aside she saw Ran scowling at her, his eyes almost black with temper. But then, as his gaze wandered down over the outlines of her upper body, all too clearly visible under the sodden cotton, his expression changed, the fierce anger being replaced by a look which strangely elated yet at the same time terrified her even more.

A burst of water almost knocked her off balance and she lurched against him. He muttered something, then dragged her into his arms, at the same time swinging her round violently, so that he was taking the full force of the jets on his back. His mouth, warm and hard, came down on hers, demanding entry which she could not deny. Her lips parted and he thrust his tongue between them, seeking the sweetness of her mouth.

Half lying, half kneeling in the water and almost dazed by the rhythmic pounding of the jets, Mellie closed her eyes, all her senses heightened, so that she could only taste him, smell his male scent, feel the taut silkiness of his wet body against hers, warm and potent. In her head she could hear the gallop of her heartbeats as her blood sang in her ears, making her reel dizzily, and with a muffled moan of pleasure she raked her fingers up his back to fasten on handfuls of his hair.

Through the wet fabric of her suit she felt him slide one hand down into the small of her back, slowly, lingeringly over the contours of her spine, then, fingers splayed, he pressed her to him——

Her eyes flew open and she tried to push him away, but he seized her roughly by the arm, pulling her back down into the water.

'What the hell's biting you?' His face was flushed, his breathing harsh.

Mellie mumbled something through her swollen lips.

'What?'

'I said—you haven't got anything on!' she yelled, though without looking at him.

'Well, what do you expect? I wasn't exactly planning on visitors, having given strict orders that I wasn't to be disturbed.'

'Oh, don't blame Mrs Pearson,' she said hastily. 'I came in through the side door.'

'You mean the one I locked myself an hour ago,' he said with heavy irony. 'It's all right,' as she tried to protest, 'I shan't dismiss her. Knowing you, I don't imagine you gave her overmuch choice—but you'll kindly remember in future, if you know what's good for you, that is, that when I give orders I expect them to be obeyed.'

This time he made no attempt to stop her as she hauled herself out, to stand, miserably angry, water cascading off her on to the champagne-coloured tiles and trying unostentatiously to ease her sodden clothes away from her skin. Ugh, it felt as though someone had wrapped her tightly in cold, slimy face-flannels!

She heard Ran getting out and hastily averted her eyes as he eased past her and turned off the hose tap, but she was unable to prevent her treacherous gaze from following him as he walked across to where a navy towelling robe was draped over a rail. He must have been using the new sunbeds, she thought inconsequentially, as she took in the smooth, tanned skin, encasing the rippling muscles beneath it as neatly as a glove would fit a hand.

Mellie was still watching him, her awareness of the lines of his body heightened still further when he reached down a towel and casually knotted it low on his hips. Suddenly he turned to her, holding out the robe.

'Get out of those wet things,' he said brusquely.

She swallowed in a vain attempt to clear an obstruction which was blocking her throat, then clutched one hand to the front of her suit.

'N-no, it's all right. I'm——'

'——a bloody fool. I know that. But get yourself out of them or, if you prefer, I'll get you out of them.'

When she still hesitated, he tossed the robe down on to the bench and advanced purposefully towards her.

'Oh, all right,' she snapped and, ducking past him, snatched up the robe and shut herself in one of the cubicles, slamming the door hard.

She stared at her misty reflection in the square of beaten copper which served as a mirror. What a sight—her hair looking as though it were glued to her head, her suit still clinging to her like a second skin, and her eyes—sparking with a volatile mixture of half anger, half terror at what she had unleashed.

She peeled off the suit and flung it on the floor, together with her bra and pants, in a pathetic heap. It was probably ruined—and it was all Ran's fault, she thought resentfully. She didn't quite know how, but it definitely *was* his fault. Behind her, the door opened.

'Oh, go away!' she exclaimed in alarm, and caught what just might have been a soft laugh as a hand tossed a towel in at her, then withdrew. A moment later she heard a shower running.

She scrubbed impatiently at her skin with the towel. Her anger and sense of righteous grievance had been cooling since her headlong fall into the whirlpool, but that soft laugh had set it simmering again.

When she emerged, Ran, safely back in his own towel, was vigorously drying his hair. Through the folds of towel he caught sight of her in the doorway and his hands stilled for a moment as his eyes lingered over her slender shape, swathed in the expanse of navy robe. Instinctively Mellie's hand went to the neckline and she drew the edges together more firmly, pleating the fabric with nervous fingers. Their eyes met, then he looked past her, his lips tightening, and he brushed back his unruly hair into some sort of order.

'Now, perhaps you'll be good enough to enlighten me as to what the hell's going on? Was it your idea of a joke, or something?'

He was so sure, so confident of himself. 'No, it wasn't, actually,' she flung at him. 'But perhaps, knowing your perverted sense of humour, it *was* your idea of a little joke to get me the push from my job!'

She felt a momentary glimmer of inner satisfaction as she saw him give a faint start, but then his eyes narrowed to steely-grey points. 'What do you mean?'

'You know very well what I mean. You—persuaded Chris to dismiss me.'

'Whoever gave you that idea?'

'Chris, as a matter of fact. I met her in Birmingham today. Well?' Ran was gazing at her, his face an inscrutable mask. 'Surely your devious mind can think of something, or aren't you going to deny it?'

He shrugged carelessly. 'Why should I? It's the truth.'

'So you admit it.' Mellie gave a mirthless laugh. 'And you'll also admit, I trust, that you knew, the night of the party after you'd—when you said you just might have heard something about it. Of course you knew,' the full extent of Ran's perfidy hit her square in the midriff, 'and you didn't just know—you'd set the whole thing up!'

The fingers of one hand were balling up into a fist, and Ran said very softly, 'You weren't thinking of hitting me, I'm sure, Melissa, but—don't.' There was a sibilant threat behind the words, but this only acted as a red rag.

'Oh, yes, and if I do, what then?'

'Well,' he surveyed her insolently, 'first, I shall tear off that wrap. Then I shall throw you back in the whirlpool, and then——' he paused.

'Go on—you don't frighten me.' She was lying through her teeth, but her temper would not be denied.

'——and then I shall jump in after you, and finish what I started a few minutes ago. Don't tell me you'd be unwilling, Mellie—that maidenly act just won't work with me. After all, any man will do, won't he?'

Mellie gasped in outrage, her fingers curling with the desire to leap at him and claw the arrogance from his face, but instead she thrust her hands fiercely into the pockets of the robe.

'Oh, but you're quite wrong there, Ran.' Her voice was sharp with splinters, although her lower lip trembled slightly. 'Any man—except one.' She put all the venom she was capable of into those final words and she had, just for a second, the satisfaction of seeing his lips tighten as though she had physically struck him.

'But do tell me,' she seized this momentary advantage, 'why did you set it up? Why did you pretend that offering me a job was an out-of-the-blue brainwave? You really did fool me, you know.' Her voice wavered and she stopped, then went on, her tone hardening again. 'How you must have enjoyed your little joke at my expense—or was it gratuitous cruelty? You really do like to have the whole world jumping through your hoops, don't you?' His dark brows snapped down into a scowl, but she continued, 'Denis, for instance—just what do you have on him?'

He shrugged. 'That's no concern of yours. Let's

just say he owed me a favour from way back. I merely told him it was pay-day.'

For an instant she glimpsed the total, driving ruthlessness of the man, and could barely suppress a shudder.

'Anyway,' he went on, 'if you'll just stop spitting and snarling like a wildcat long enough to think, you'll admit that I was doing you a good turn.' Ignoring her laugh of cold disbelief, he continued, 'Chris is small-time. You've got brains and common sense—though it's not always apparent—and were ideal for my enterprise. So when I heard you telling Olivia that you might be offered a partnership, I knew I had to act fast.'

Melissa gasped in fury. 'How dare you! How dare you decide what's best for me? Just stay out of my life, will you? No one, but no one, arranges it for me—do you hear?'

'I hear you perfectly,' Ran's voice was arctic-chill, 'but if you'll just close your mouth for a few seconds and make use of your brain instead, you'll admit that I was right. In case it hasn't registered, you've handled all the work I've heaped on you more than competently, and what's more, you've given every appearance of enjoying it.'

He was right, of course. She *had* been enjoying every hectic minute, every new challenge, every chance to make her own decisions, until—she gnawed her lower lip. Oh, why had some malign fate had to arrange for her to bump into Chris like that, to drag her out of her blissful ignorance? She had been happy—for so long as she hadn't known about Ran's cold-blooded manipulations—but she couldn't stay, not now.

Ran had outmanoeuvred her, controlled her exactly as though she were an inert puppet. That ruthless, almost physical drive frightened her. Just as a juggernaut will catch hold of its victim and destroy it under its unstoppable momentum, so Ran would snatch her up, crush her and, when it suited him, abandon her without the slightest compunction.

'You realise, of course, that I shall have to leave, now that I know this.' She was pleased with how impersonal she sounded. 'I'm handing in my notice, as of this moment. If you wish, I shall continue with you until——'

'Oh, for heaven's sake, Melissa, don't talk such bloody nonsense! You're not leaving.'

'I most certainly am—and there's nothing you can do about it. I didn't sign a fifty-year contract, you know. Aunt Livy's better—once she gets back from Cornwall, she won't need me—so I'm giving notice——'

'Oh, shut up,' Ran yelled at her, 'or I'll put you over my knee and give you a hiding you won't forget in a hurry! I do mean it, Melissa,' he added menacingly, and she subsided hastily into a sullen silence.

'That's better,' he continued, in a marginally milder tone. 'But just don't provoke me any more.'

She jutted her chin and was just trying unsuccessfully to beat down his haughty gaze with one of chill disdain, when the effect was utterly ruined by two tremendous sneezes.

He put his hand on her arm. 'You're cold.'

'I'm perfectly all right,' she snarled. 'I'll return

your robe in the morning. Let go my arm, will you!'
as his fingers tightened on it.

'Be half-way reasonable for once. It's pouring with
rain. Listen.'

For the first time Mellie became aware of the
raindrops pattering heavily against the glass roof
panels.

'I shall be quite all right. I've got Aunt Livy's
car.'

'There's no need for you to go.' Ran, standing in
the doorway, effectively shutting off her escape, no
doubt thought he could now afford to be relaxed,
even moderately affable. 'It's a filthy night, you're all
on your own at the cottage——' she toyed briefly with
the tempting notion of telling him that she wouldn't
be alone, then reluctantly decided not '—so come
through to my flat. I'll put your clothes in the tumble-
drier. In any case, I wanted to talk to you.'

'About my trip today? Can't it wait till tomorrow?'

'No, I'm afraid it can't wait. Anyway, have you had
anything to eat?'

'Well, I had a few sandwiches at lunchtime——'

'I'll do you a meal, then. Nothing spectacular—just
a steak.'

Just a steak. All at once, hunger was gnawing at her
vitals. Ran was already turning away, as though the
whole thing was settled.

'Do I have any choice?' she called after him, still not
quite ready to give in.

'Not really. You either come willingly, or——' He
left the threat incomplete.

Well, she could try and outsprint him to her car . . .
Right now, though, her stomach was more concerned

with food than another fight, and besides, she thought gloomily as she picked up her bag and followed him down the winding passage, Ran was like water on a stone. He was wearing her down into a weary acceptance.

But, after all, it *was* a free country—and however much he might resemble them physically, he was not one of those Border lords with unquestioned life-and-death powers—and she most definitely was not one of his serfs. She would say nothing more tonight, but she was still going to give in her notice tomorrow . . .

He had turned and was waiting for her, so she dropped her gaze to hide the glint of defiance in her green eyes, hoping that he would take her meekly lowered head as a gesture of surrender.

CHAPTER FIVE

MELISSA knew that, as well as having the newer part of the Manor refurbished as the conference centre, Ran was having the small square stone tower renovated for his own private quarters, but until now she had not penetrated beyond the hallowed portals. So now she looked around her in frank curiosity as he ushered her into a small lobby piled high with boxes of rubbish and what seemed like dozens of glass-fronted cases, filled with some long-dead collector's trophies: huge butterflies with multi-coloured, fragile wings and stuffed animals which looked at her with horrible dead eyes, so that she shuddered.

'Sorry not to bring you in by the front door,' he remarked, 'but I've shoved all the rest of the junk from the last six centuries in there, so that the workmen can get stuck into my apartment.'

'Why have you decided to live in this part of the house?' Until now, it had seemed to her more fitting for him to have taken part of the elegant eighteenth-century extension as his private territory.

Ran gave her a slanting smile. 'Well, for some strange reason I feel more at home here.'

And yes, she thought, he was right—somehow he was more suited to this stone keep, with its hard, uncompromising lines and frowning battlements.

Clinging on to a rope, which served as the only

78

banister, she followed him up an endless spiral staircase, the stone treads worn down. The staircase gave one final twist, Ran flicked a light switch, and she gave a gasp of astonishment at the sight of the huge room they were standing in. It took up the whole of the first floor, apart from one end, where, through a half-open door, she glimpsed pine kitchen units. The main outer wall had at some time been stripped back to the stone, but the other three were still covered in carved linenfold panelling, which glowed honey-gold under the lights. Mellie put up a hand and softly stroked it, the wood warm under her touch.

'Like it?' Ran was standing beside her. 'They've done a good job—it was covered with stuff like black treacle when I first forced my way in here, and all the ceilings were covered with filthy, crumbling plaster. I've had them taken back to the original beams.'

Beautiful pieces of antique furniture were placed around the room, and there was an enormous, ceiling-high stone hearth at each end. One had a pile of logs in the fire basket, but Ran led the way to the far end, where a huge, comfortable-looking blue-green corduroy sofa and matching chairs were grouped around a more practical cast-iron gas fire.

He stooped to light it, then, with a swift glance at her bare legs and feet, said briskly, 'You still look cold. You'd better have a hot shower, and I'll find you some warm things to get into.'

The stone staircase led on up and she followed him to an equally large bedroom, which was dominated by a massive four-poster bed.

He saw her staring at it and laughed. 'Yes, it's the

genuine article—although I don't know whether Queen Elizabeth actually slept here. It's one of the few pieces that was worth rescuing.' He paused, then added, 'You'd be surprised how comfortable it is.'

She smiled uncertainly, not at all sure how she was supposed to react, but at the same time feeling faint resentment stir in her once more. Ran was so completely at ease here, on his own territory, while conversely she was feeling more uncomfortable by the second.

She followed him through to the bathroom, all pristine white and yellow with mahogany fittings. He lifted some pale yellow bath towels from a cupboard. 'Right, it's all yours. I'll look some clothes out for you. Oh, by the way, don't decide to have a bath—they're having problems plumbing it in and,' he added meaningfully, 'I'd hate to have water cascading over me yet again this evening.' He held out his hand for the towel in which Mellie had wrapped her wet clothes. 'I'll have those.'

Gingerly she removed the sodden jacket and skirt and handed them to him.

'Now the rest,' he said firmly, so she had no alternative but to part with the bedraggled little scraps of lace.

When he had gone, she had a shower, then wrapped herself in one of the bath towels. There was a wall-mounted hair-drier beside the bathroom cabinet; as she dried her wet, tangled hair, she opened it, a feeling of intense curiosity suddenly overcoming her scruples, and inspected the expensive-looking toiletries. She flipped open one bottle and sniffed it. Yes, that was the aftershave Ran always used, that faint sensuous aroma of musky sandalwood.

Feeling slightly ashamed, all at once, of her prying, she firmly closed the cabinet door and, still wrapped in the towel, went back to the bedroom. Laid out on the massive bed was a red sweatshirt and a pair of white cord trousers. They were both far too big for her, of course, but as she surveyed herself in the mirror she felt grateful for their all-enveloping bagginess, and in any case, when she had rolled up the sleeves and the hem of the trousers, she didn't look too bad—even if she still had some of that bedraggled orphan-in-the-storm look.

She found Ran downstairs in the kitchen. He had changed into a black tracksuit which, under the subtly concealed lighting, made him look vaguely threatening, even faintly demonic. One end of a long pine table was laid for a meal and he was at the other end, mixing a dressing for the salad while the steaks sizzled under the grill.

His eyes flicked over her, taking in her slight body swathed in his clothes, and momentarily she glimpsed in them an expression which made her feel shyly ill at ease again, but he merely gestured her to a pine stool, poured red wine from an already opened bottle into a glass and pushed it across to her.

'Now be quiet,' he commanded. 'I don't like women in my kitchen, particularly women who can cook.'

Mellie, only too glad to obey, sipped the fruity wine and watched covertly as Ran, with competent

swiftness, finished the salad, dished up the
succulent-looking steaks and fetched hot rolls from
the oven.

As they ate, their conversation was sporadic, Ran
lapsing into frequent silences, and Mellie, all her
senses conscious of him sitting just across the table
from her, so close that every time she straightened
her legs they brushed against his, was more than
happy to keep the silences going. Several times,
though, when she glanced up she caught his grey
eyes fixed on her, a brooding expression in them, and
then she would hastily glue her gaze to her plate
again for at least five minutes.

Cheese and a fruit bowl followed, then Ran pushed
his chair back and switched on the coffee percolator,
but when she began stacking the dishes he stopped
her impatiently. 'Leave them. I'll see to them
later, when you've gone. Go on through by the
fire.'

At one corner of the stone hearth there was a fat
floor cushion, its soft bluey-green paisley cover
picking up the shade of the sofa and chairs. She
plumped down on it, her chin on her knees, her bare
toes padding at the crisply curling sheepskin rug that
lay in front of the fire, and let her eyes wander about
the room. The furniture was a mish-mash of periods
and styles, yet the whole room—the modern prints,
the faded rose-pink Persian carpet, the huge old
copper jug on the Sheraton table, brimming with
white narcissi and gold wallflowers, which were
filling the air with intoxicating sweetness
—everything jelled into a harmonious, restful
whole.

But, in spite of the warmth of the fire and the mellowing effect of the wine, she herself was feeling thoroughly on edge, like a twitching cat. There was something in Ran's manner tonight—she couldn't quite define it—which was making her increasingly uneasy. Up until now, ever since she'd begun working for him, he had scrupulously observed an impersonal employer/employee relationship, but tonight there was a subtle difference . . . He'd clearly got over his outburst of temper when she had hosed him; he was calm, absolutely in control of himself, and yet maybe that scene in the whirlpool had been the catalyst for this change, so that now she felt, in some intangible way, as though he was reaching out to her, encircling her, drawing her inexorably towards him . . .

As Ran set down the tray of coffee on a low table, Mellie did her best to shake off her disturbing thoughts, even forcing a smile.

'This is a lovely room.'

'Yes, I'm rather proud of it. I designed it myself—I wanted to make this a place to unwind in, somewhere where I could be wholly myself.'

But what *is* yourself? Mellie wanted to ask, but instead she said, 'Cream, please, but no sugar.'

Under cover of sipping the fragrant coffee, she looked about the room again. So Ran had built it round himself. What a man of surprises he was! And yet, coupled with his toughness, there had always been an elegance about him, a pride and consciousness of his own rightness that, whatever his external poverty, had always made him carry himself like a young Border princeling.

And now, sprawled negligently in the chair facing her, running one finger idly around the rim of his cup as he frowned into the depths of his black coffee——

Mellie's throat was suddenly dry and her hand was shaking so much that some of the coffee slopped over into the saucer. She set her cup down jerkily, this time spilling the hot liquid on her hand, though she was scarcely conscious of the tingling pain. This scene of shared intimacy had, all at once, brought back to her, with a searing clarity that she had thought long buried, that other brief moment of intimacy she had shared with Ran eight years ago. How she had loved him then, had longed with all her being to be always with him, uniting her whole life with his as she was now sharing these few fleeting moments.

But those feelings were dead now; she herself—through her own weakness—had killed them, and all her instincts told her that for her own sake, for her own sanity, there was no future—absolutely none—in allowing that love to be reborn. If needs be, she would even have to learn something of Ran's own ruthlessness—although whether she really had it in her . . .

She swallowed down the rest of her coffee and reached for her bag. When he glanced at her, she said huskily, 'I really must go, Ran. Aunt Livy sometimes rings up last thing, to see if I've managed to kill off her precious plants yet.' She smiled faintly, but he did not respond, only watched her. 'Thank you for the meal—I can find my own way down——'

'You're not going yet, Melissa.'

The words were spoken quietly enough, but the undercurrent, faint though it was, stilled her just for a moment, then she was scrambling awkwardly to her feet. Out of the corner of her eye, she saw Ran put down his cup and uncoil himself like a steel spring.

'I said you aren't going yet.' His tone was almost conversational and he made no move to touch her, but the hairs on the nape of her neck pinpricked. 'Olivia's rung up already today, while you were out——'

'Oh, how is she?'

'Absolutely fine,' he said briefly. 'So sit down. I want to talk to you—remember?'

He gestured towards the sofa and Mellie sank into it with just one mutinous glance. He threw himself down beside her, one arm laid carelessly along the back, his fingers almost but not quite brushing her shoulder.

'Well?' Her inner struggle to appear calm put a metallic edge to her voice. 'What do you want to talk about? That kitchen designer's coming again tomorrow——'

'Marry me, Melissa.'

'What?' She stared at him, the incredulous astonishment hugely dilating her green eyes.

'I said—I want you to marry me.'

Just for a moment there was a surge of utterly ridiculous joy, but then almost simultaneously ice-cold reality returned, bringing her back to sanity.

'B-but you don't love me.'

Ran laughed harshly. 'Love! What's that? There's

been precious little of that in my life—or even earlier. There was a distinct absence of that commodity at my conception—or so I've always been led to believe. No, I'm afraid love's an emotion I've taken very good care to steer clear of. But,' his face twisted in cynical amusement, 'I'll go down on one knee, Melissa, if that's all that's bothering you.' The biting edge to his voice jolted her out of her daze. 'I've had very good experience of what loving you means, remember? That night when you walked away from me, I wanted to run after you, shout *you're mine, damn you*, beg you to stay, but you didn't. So then, that day in the wood, when I saw you again, I made up my mind that this time I would have you, and nothing would stop me.'

'No!'

Nausea was clawing at her insides. Revenge—that was what he wanted. She stared at him, as though mesmerised by his eyes, cold and hard as basalt. This was what everything had been leading up to. All unknown and unsuspected, Ran had been prowling around her like a huge forest tiger, gradually circling in for the kill. She tried to speak, but her throat was clenched tight. Useless anyway to protest, to try to make him understand that she'd been a young, helpless girl.

She bent her head, to watch her fingers endlessly twisting in her lap. 'Please, Ran,' she said in a low voice, 'I can't marry you—you must see that. It's quite impossible. All you want is revenge, not a marriage.'

'Revenge?' His face twisted. 'Don't you think I haven't taken revenge on every woman I've known for not being you? No, Mellie, it's you I want—no one else will satisfy me. You're beautiful, desirable, and you're going to belong to me.'

'No—no, I'm not!' she burst out wildly. 'If you just want something beautiful and desirable, you can buy yourself a few more rugs or pictures. You feel no more for me than—than that collector felt for one of those lovely butterflies downstairs. It would be no different, not at all—the poor, helpless thing caught in a net, its struggles growing feebler all the time, then pinned up as a trophy. And that's all I'd be. You—you might as well put me in a glass case and have done with it!'

Her voice was shaking, but when she looked imploringly at Ran, he was leaning back, completely unruffled, regarding her over the bridge of his fingers.

'Oh, no, I don't intend to put you in a glass case.' His voice held a soft thread of menace. 'Such a waste of a lovely young body! No, the place I have in mind for you is—somewhere else entirely.' Then, as her eyes darkened in horrified suspicion, 'That bed upstairs.'

Mellie sprang to her feet. 'I've told you—I won't marry you!' She was shouting now, but Ran merely shook his head sadly.

'Now that's—unfortunate.'

'Yes, well, I'm sorry, but you must see——'

'I hoped you'd come to me of your own free will. It's such a pity.'

'W-what do you mean—it's a pity?'

'Your aunt—she seems much better.'

'Aunt Livy? Oh yes, she is.' She was momentarily

thrown off balance by Ran's abrupt change of topic,
but now she gratefully babbled on, 'She's having a
wonderful time staying with Arnold—she's been
helping him plan a new area for his camellias. But
she's looking forward to coming home——'

'Hmm, that's the impression I got. So it would be
such a shame if she had to move out of the cottage.'

The coldly chipped words fell into the room like
fragments of ice. Mellie went very still, then, before
her legs could buckle under her, she sank down again
on to the sofa.

'Just what does that mean?' Her voice was totally
devoid of expression.

'Oh, I'm sure you understand.'

'No, I don't—I won't!' She just could not bring
herself to confront the dreadful suspicion that was
beginning to uncoil in her mind.

'I'll have to spell it out for you, then. Your aunt is
one of my tenants—her cottage is part of the estate,
and I'm afraid I need a house for my new land agent.
If he were a bachelor he could make do with a flatlet
in the Manor, but,' his gesture conveyed heartfelt
regret, 'he's married—there's a young child.'

Mellie was gazing at him in stunned disbelief. 'But
you can't—you just can't do this to her! She's lived
there for as long as I can remember. She—she made
that garden out of an old meadow. Please, Ran! I—I
thought you liked her.'

'I'm afraid there's no room for sentiment where
business is concerned.' She eyed him narrowly, but
then, as she saw the adamantine sheen in his eyes,
she went very pale.

'You mean it, you really mean it, don't you? But

can't you see? It—it would kill her to have to leave!'

'Oh, I think you're getting hysterical now, Mellie. But if anything—unfortunate should occur, I don't suppose you'd want it on your conscience.'

'*My* conscience! Why should it be on mine? If you had one ounce of——'

'Well, you see, Mellie, it's up to you whether you're prepared to take that chance. But the remedy is entirely in your hands.'

His eyes held hers and she felt a bleak, despairing hopelessness wash through her. So that was it, finally out in the open.

'You mean,' her voice was shaking again, though whether with anger or fear she was not sure, 'Aunt Livy stays in her cottage, if I agree to marry you.'

Ran nodded. 'She stays—and with a life tenancy.'

'It's blackmail—you realise that? What a chip off the old block you are, after all, Ran! Your father would have been really proud of you.' Her lip curled derisively. 'So Dad was right about you all——'

'Shut up!' His face darkened and for one terrifying moment she thought he was going to strike her, but he merely said, 'Well? What is it to be?'

Her eyes roamed frantically around the enormous room, seeking some way of escape, and then they fell on the telephone.

'I'll tell my father. You'll never get away with this, I swear! In fact, I'm going to ring him right now.'

But even as she tensed to jump to her feet, he snatched hold of her arm, forcing it back relentlessly until she subsided.

'Don't bother, Mellie.' His purring voice grated in her ear. 'Unlike that last time, I hold all the cards now, not your precious father.'

Naked triumph gleamed in his eyes and Mellie realised, with a despairing lurch of her stomach, that, whatever Ran might say, for him finally to get the better of her father would give an added piquancy to his victory.

She glared at him, gnawing her underlip. She *couldn't* marry him—and yet the alternative was unthinkable. Oh heavens, she was beginning to feel like a fly enmeshed in a sticky web! Her struggles were inward, not physical now, and yet there sat Ran, every bit as lethal as a dangerous spider, watching her as dispassionately as though he were sizing her up for his next victim. It was useless, quite useless to beg for mercy—for Aunt Livy, or herself.

'All right, Ran,' she said tonelessly, 'I'll marry you. I just hope you come to think you've got a bargain, that's all.'

'A bargain?' With deliberate insolence, he let his eyes wander over her body. 'Oh, I think so.'

She fumbled on the floor for her bag and stood up. She realised suddenly that she was still wearing his clothes, but she couldn't bear to wait while he fetched hers. She had to get away—now.

Over her shoulder, she flung at him. 'You'll let me know when the happy event is to take place, I trust. I'd hate to miss it.'

'Friday.'

Mellie stopped dead, and turned slowly to face

him. 'You mean—*this* Friday?'

'Yes, I got a special licence this morning.'

She stared down at him. Men like Ran should carry a public health warning: Danger—keep clear. He was still watching her coolly, as though to gauge her reaction, and for a second she almost jumped at his throat, but she knew well enough who would come off worse in any physical mauling, and she wasn't going to give him that added satisfaction. Cold disdain was her best—her only weapon now.

'You must have been very sure of yourself—of your charms!' she allowed herself to spit out the final three words.

'No, Mellie, not of my charms.' Just for a moment she saw a flicker in his grey eyes of—pain? Surely not, for he went on cynically, 'I knew that if it came to it, you wouldn't be able to refuse. You're a tender-hearted little thing.'

'I see.'

She nodded, as though assimilating his words. Well, she thought, we'll have to see just how tender-hearted I am where you're concerned, won't we?

In the doorway she stopped, though without turning. Ran was right behind her; she felt his breath on her neck.

'Tell me,' she said conversationally, 'how does it feel to be marrying a woman who hates you?'

But before she could escape down the stairs, he had swung her round and was turning her face up to his. With the tip of his thumb, he brushed across her full lower lip in a slow, sensuous movement, so that in spite of herself she felt her stomach muscles tighten.

'But you don't hate me, Mellie, you know you

don't.'

She wrenched her head away. 'Yes, I do!' she all but shrieked at him, then, breaking free, she tore headlong down the stone staircase, round and round, until she was dizzy and sobbing for breath.

CHAPTER SIX

'MUMMY—over here!'

Mellie waved as she caught sight of her mother coming through into the passenger terminal at Birmingham Airport.

'Hello, darling.'

As Mrs Grant hugged and kissed her daughter, Mellie looked past her shoulder. 'But where's Daddy?'

'Well, actually, Mellie,' her mother wasn't quite meeting her eyes, 'he—well, he hasn't been too well lately, so we decided it was best—all this rush would have been a bit much for him. But he sends his love, of course.'

She looked appealingly at her and Mellie stared blindly at her for a moment, trying to swallow down the tight stone that was lodging painfully in her throat. Of course, she should have guessed. The same evening after that traumatic scene with Ran, she'd stumbled into the cottage, almost too dazed to think, but had somehow calmed herself sufficiently to phone her parents with the news that their only daughter was to be married, in just four days' time, to Ranulf Owen.

Her father had been first incredulous, then hostile, then finally coldly formal. 'Well, you're old enough to know your own mind, I suppose . . .'

She saw her mother's anxious blue eyes fixed on her and managed a weak smile. 'Please don't worry, Mummy, I quite understand. Now, would you like a cup of tea, or shall we get straight back? I've got Aunt Livy's car.' She was chattering brightly, in an effort to break the tension. 'Arnold's driving her up. He's staying at the Morville Arms tonight . . .'

'Just who is this Arnold, anyway?'

'Oh, he's rather a sweetie. He's the one who . . .'

The explanations helped carry them on towards Shropshire, and the whole journey seemed compounded of short bursts of stilted conversation, punctuated by long silences. It was obvious that her mother was torn by guilt and embarrassment over her father's absence, and Mellie thought ironically that it was tempting to turn to her and say, 'Look, don't give it another thought. This is such a travesty of a wedding anyway that Daddy's staying away in a huff just completes it.'

As she drove past the village church, she saw Mrs Pearson and another woman going in, laden with sheaves of white gladioli and marguerites. They were decorating the church for her wedding the next morning . . . The dreadful enormity of what she was about to do swept over her. She drew in her breath to speak, torn apart by the longing to pour out the whole horrible story, but then she bit back the words as Ran's voice re-echoed in her mind. 'I hold the trump cards now, not your precious father.'

And it was true. This was just between Ran and her—everyone else was a mere, unknowing onlooker, and would have to stay that way. If Aunt

Livy should even suspect the real reason why she was going through with this mockery of a marriage . . . No, she was on her own, with no one to turn to for help or even understanding.

At the cottage, she made a pot of tea, conscious all the time of her mother's worried eyes on her, and as she set down the tray on the kitchen table, Mrs Grant said abruptly, 'You are quite sure, aren't you, darling? I mean, it's not too late——' Her voice trailed away into doubtful silence.

'Perfectly sure.' Mellie's voice was completely unemotional, but her mother relaxed and gave her daughter a faint smile.

'Yes, well, although——' she hesitated, caught Mellie's eye, then went on valiantly, 'although your father was never all that keen on Ran, I always thought he was a nice lad——' Ran—nice? Oh well, even a puff-adder must have a few doting admirers somewhere '—and I'm sure he's grown into a fine young man.'

Mellie opened her mouth to shriek, No, he hasn't, he's utterly vile and I loathe him, but instead she merely said, 'Would you like another biscuit? I know you like these chocolate digestives.'

The telephone rang. Ran no doubt, twitching the noose, making sure she was safely back in the net. But instead,

'Mellie, is that you?'

'Aunt Livy—where are you?'

'Stuck in a village on the outskirts of Bristol.' Her normally calm, unflappable aunt sounded quietly frantic. 'Arnold's car's broken down, but the garage man has promised to get it repaired first thing

tomorrow morning. The wedding's not till midday,
is it? That's what Ran said when he rang to tell
me——'

'Yes.'

'Well, I promise we'll be there. Arnold says he'll
hire a car if necessary.'

A thought suddenly struck Mellie and she said
carefully, 'Aunt Livy, Mum's here, but Daddy—he
isn't well. He hasn't come.'

'Oh, yes.' Olivia's dry tone conveyed a multitude
of meaning. She had never had much time for her
martinet of a brother-in-law.

'So I was wondering—would Arnold give me away,
do you think?'

'Mellie love, I'm sure he'll be delighted. And not to
worry—we'll be there.'

Ran did ring later and offered to take them both out
for dinner that evening, but Mellie brusquely
refused. The mere thought of him and her mother
making meaningless small talk across a gulf,
unacknowledged but infinitely wider than a
restaurant table's breadth, filled her with revulsion.
Instead, she willingly went along with her mother's
suggestion that she be in bed before ten—'after all,
darling, an early night makes a beautiful bride'—but
then lay, staring at the ceiling, until the first subdued
twitterings of the dawn chorus began.

All through the wakeful night one single thought
hammered at her mind. Years before, to be married to
Ran would have been her ultimate joy. Now she *was*
marrying him, and it was all so different. Once he
had loved her . . . 'Oh, Lissy, you must know how I

feel about you! I love you, love you, love you' . . . But
with those few faltering, cowardly words of denial,
she had killed that love, had destroyed his capacity to
love her forever. Now, too late, she knew that his
love was the most precious thing in life to her. *Too
late*. Were there any more desolate words in the
whole language . . .?

. . . She was running up an endless spiral stone
staircase, gasping for breath, her leaden footsteps
echoing off the walls. Ran was behind her—she knew
he was, she could hear him, and yet, as she turned
the last corner, he was ahead of her, staring down at
her, his arms folded, his mouth twisted in a cruel
smile of conquest. Then he put out his hands and
reached for her. 'No!' she screamed, and was
hurtling downwards into space——

The bedroom flooded with light as her mother
drew back the curtains and set down a tray of tea and
toast beside her.

'You're very pale, darling. I hope you slept
well?'

Mellie lay for a moment, feeling that tight knot
of terror unravel itself in her stomach. 'Yes, thank
you.'

When her mother had gone, she sat up in bed and
managed to force down a little of the toast by dint of
washing down every dry mouthful with tea. She
caught sight of her reflection in the dressing-table
mirror. Her mother was right—against the black hair,
her face was absolutely colourless, apart from the
dark bruises of shadows brushed under her vivid
green eyes, and there was a new tautness about her
mouth. It's my wedding day, she thought suddenly,

then, as her face began to crumple and dissolve behind a mist of tears, she jumped out of bed and went to shampoo her hair while her bath was running.

When her mother came back, Mellie was already dressed and staring listlessly down at the antique rose diamond ring which Ran had given her two days ago. As she had looked at its delicate, unflawed beauty, a sick hopelessness had invaded her mind, and for a moment she had almost begged him not to force her to go through with this, but then, as she glanced up swiftly into his face, pride had held her silent. There was no mercy in those cold eyes—not for her, at any rate.

Obediently she stood up for her mother's inspection. She had tried to tell Ran that almost any pretty dress would do these days, but he, no doubt bent on showing off his trophy, had insisted that she buy a wedding dress. Wandering round Shrewsbury, she had toyed with a rather fetching one in black silk—very appropriate, black—but finally forced her unwilling feet towards the bridal department in one of the large stores.

Now her mother gave her a watery smile. 'You look beautiful, darling. A perfect May bride.'

And when Mellie, for the first time, really looked in the mirror she stared at herself, her heart beating a little faster. Maybe it was true—that, quite simply, all brides are beautiful. And yet the white lawn fabric, as fine as silk, the plain rounded neckline, and slightly gathered skirt which ended in a small train, set off perfectly her dainty slenderness, while her mother's veil of Honiton lace, which all the family brides for the last hundred years had worn, framed the rather fragile, elfin beauty of her face. She smiled tremulously at her reflection and saw the faint frown lines between her arched brows dissolve, just for a moment, into an expression of starry-eyed radiance.

'It's such a pity not having any bridesmaids.' Her mother was sounding faintly reproachful. 'Joan's twins would have looked lovely, or some of your school friends. If only we could have let more people know, but you were—well, in such a hurry. What people will think, I dread to imagine!' She was almost wailing now. 'This just isn't the sort of wedding your father and I——'

'Well, it can't be helped.' Anger with Ran for manipulating her into this impossible situation was almost choking Mellie, so that she could not trust herself to say anything more.

'And Livy's cutting it very fine.' Mrs Grant shot back the cuff of her pink flowered silk suit and clicked her tongue. 'Why on earth she couldn't come up by train, I do not know.'

The wedding cars were already waiting when finally, at ten minutes to twelve, Livy and Arnold arrived, amid a welter of frenzied apologies and explanations. Her aunt was wearing her one moderately elegant outfit, her felt hat slipping rakishly over one ear, but Arnold was looking surprisingly well groomed in a charcoal grey suit.

While her mother and aunt were whisked off in their car, he burrowed in the boot of the Cortina and emerged clutching a single white camellia flower, its stem carefully enclosed in wet tissue.

'It's a bit the worse for wear, I'm afraid, after the delay, but we—Livy and I thought you might like it.' With a jerky little gesture, he handed it to her. 'It's a new variety I've just developed. I—er—thought I'd call it Melissa's Wedding.'

Mellie looked down at the flower, with its pure white satiny petals and golden centre. Melissa's Wedding—a beautiful name for what should have been the most beautiful day of her life . . .

'Oh, it's lovely, Arnold! Thank you,' was all she could manage as, her eyes brimming with tears, she turned blindly away to tuck it into her simply posy of white freesias.

There was a knot of onlookers at the lych-gate and the church was crowded with villagers, but she saw them only with the very edge of her conscious mind. Ran, in a dark grey suit and white shirt, and framed in a dazzle of light from one of the stained glass windows, was standing at the chancel steps, watching her as she came towards him on Arnold's arm. His eyes were intent on them, and he was frowning slightly. Of course—her mother probably hadn't dared tell him that the bride's father was suffering from a diplomatic illness.

She was close enough now to see the expression in his eyes. Cool triumph—perhaps even he had had a moment's doubt that she really would go through with this hollow farce—but behind that, something else, something which made her all at once begin to vibrate softly inside, as though he had set a bell swinging slowly, silently.

'Dearly beloved, we are gathered together . . .'

Mellie tore her eyes from Ran, grateful for the veil to screen the sudden, intense blush which had fired her cheeks . . .

The wide gold band, symbol of her final subjection as Ran slipped it on to her finger . . . the register . . . photographs . . . laughter—other people's, not hers . . . Ran shielding her from a volley of rice and rose petals as they climbed into the car . . . the silent drive, mercifully short, to the Manor . . . standing stiffly beside him, that bright, artificial smile tacked to her face, as they received their guests . . .

The wedding breakfast, the toasts, in the panelled dining-room with its elegant apricot and brown décor—the décor which she, just weeks earlier, had so lovingly planned . . . at last escaping upstairs with her mother and aunt to change ready for her departure on honeymoon . . .

'Darling, why ever didn't you tell me?' Mrs Grant was smiling at her in mock reproach. 'They say that one wedding makes another, but I would never have——' Mellie roused herself from her reverie to look in blank puzzlement from her mother to her aunt, who was all at once blushing pinkly. 'You *did* know, didn't you?' her mother added.

'I don't think she does, Sarah.' Olivia was looking at her closely. 'Ran hasn't told you, has he?'

Mellie's fingers had stilled on the tie-belt of her casual peach-coloured linen shirtwaister, and fine needle-points of ugly suspicion were pricking at her mind. 'Told me what, Aunt Livy?'

'Why, that Arnold and I are getting married. He asked me earlier this week and—well——' the normally down-to-earth Olivia was now looking almost girlishly coy, 'I said yes. I rang you at once to tell you, but you were in Birmingham, so I phoned Ran instead. After all, as his tenant, I needed to let him know.'

'Let him know——?' Mellie hardly recognised her own voice.

'That I'll be leaving the cottage, of course. Arnold has this absolutely beautiful house, and the climate is perfect for camellias. He's developed some wonderful new species and we're . . .'

Mellie clenched her fingers so that the nails bit into her palms, as she forced down the urge to scream, But you can't, you can't! You don't understand—you don't know what I've done. I've ruined my whole life for you!

'It's marvellous news, isn't it, darling?'

She sensed her mother watching her rather curiously, and somehow managed to say, 'Yes, it is. I'm so glad for you both.' And she hugged her aunt, then kissed her cheek.

Minutes later, beside Ran's grey Jaguar, the farewells . . . Aunt Livy clasping her tightly. 'Be happy, Mellie. You've got a good man there—one of the best,' then behind her, Ran's drawl, 'That's what I'm always telling her, Olivia, but she doesn't seem to believe me.'

As the general laughter rang shrilly in her ears, Mellie embraced her mother, resting her head against the flowered silk to try to still her quivering lip. But then her mother whispered into her hair, 'No tears, darling, please, or I shall cry too,' so she straightened up and passively allowed Ran to hand her into the car. He slid in beside her and next moment the smiling faces, already blurred and unreal, were receding swiftly behind them.

Mellie watched yet another village flash past. Ran was driving faster all the time, though never less than skilfully, and whenever she sneaked a furtive glance at his hard profile he seemed fully engrossed on the road ahead.

The silence had lasted ever since they had left the Manor, and the longer it went on the more determined she was that she would not be the one to shatter it. And besides, the silence was feeding her anger, giving her the chance to reflect on just how Ran had duped her, had blackmailed her into marriage on a lie. Oh, he had not actually lied to her—he was far too devious for that—he'd merely cheated, manipulated her with such a ruthless abuse of her love for Aunt Livy and total disregard for her own feelings that she felt bludgeoned. She should feel anger, rage, but that, she knew, would come later—it was there, ticking between them like a time-bomb—but for now, as the miles sped past, she felt only a sick numbness creeping over her.

When they reached the motorway interchange Ran took the northbound route, and she was at last surprised into speech.

'Are we flying from Manchester?'

'We aren't flying from anywhere.'

'You mean we're staying in England?'

He nodded, and she caught a flicker of amusement round his mouth.

'But that's ridiculous!' She turned to him, her

green eyes blazing. 'You know very well I thought we were going abroad. You said, did I want to go to Mauritius, Bermuda or——'

'And you said, go where the hell you like, it's your honeymoon, not mine. So, without your expert guidance, I just had to go ahead and make the arrangements on my own.'

'Yes, the way you've arranged everything else!' she snarled. 'If I'd thought for one instant that you'd have taken any notice of my ideas, I might have given you some. But, with your twisted sense of humour, if I'd said the Seychelles, you—you'd have taken us to Lapland!'

Mellie broke off, staring tight-lipped at the road ahead. Although Ran was right—she had resolutely refused even to think of the honeymoon, much less talk about it—after his suggestions, she had tacitly assumed that he would book them in at some suitably exotic spot, and her clothes had been chosen accordingly.

Finally, however, even though every outraged fibre in her was shrieking in silent rebellion, she snapped, 'Perhaps you'd be good enough to inform me just where we *are* going—not that I care in the slightest, of course.'

'The Lake District. Do you know it?'

'Yes.'

In fact, she had rosy memories of several happy childhood holidays spent there—memories which no doubt were about to be obliterated forever. And besides—she remembered suddenly the case full of bikinis, pretty sundresses and cover-ups frantically got together for buffet lunches beside some tropical hotel pool.

'You really should have told me,' she said, a hint of sullenness in her voice. 'I just haven't got the right clothes.'

'Oh, dear, not sulking, are you? I do detest sulky women.'

'Well, that's something you're just going to have to get used to.'

As she swung round to scowl at him, she caught the tail-end of a speculative glance. Maybe he was wondering whether or not she had heard Aunt Livy's news. Her silence had perhaps led him to believe that, in the general confusion, her aunt had not had a chance to tell her. She smiled savagely to herself. If he really thought that, he was in for a nasty shock!

She could feel the rage welling up in her now, white-hot, and she longed to hurl herself at him, but some small residue of caution was holding her in check. The fast lane of the motorway at the height of the Friday evening exodus was neither the place nor the time to start taking Ran apart at the seams, but very soon now, she would—oh, she would!

She risked another glance. How smug he looked—that unutterable smugness of the self-confident, arrogant male. The corner of his mouth was twitching. Damn him—he knew she was watching him; probably thought she was secretly admiring his dazzling good looks. But as she continued to look at him from under her lashes, the insidious, hateful awareness of just how handsome, how potently attractive he was began to snake itself into her mind and she wrenched her head away, closed her eyes tightly and took refuge in a feigned sleep until long after she had sensed him turn off the motorway.

They dined at a red-brick hotel high up above Windermere, where Ran had booked a table looking out over the lake. Mellie told herself fiercely that she was not at all inhibited by the atmosphere of quiet luxury or the unobtrusive but ever-watchful service, but as long as they were here she certainly could not allow herself to indulge in anything so vulgar as a stand-up shouting match.

Instead, she had to make do with all but ignoring him, resolutely fixing her gaze on the grey-blue waters of the lake, bounded by the rising fells turned to a soft green by the early evening sunlight. As she sat, her spoon poised over her avocado pear liberally coated with a thyme-flavoured dressing, the memory of one particular holiday came back to her suddenly, piercingly bitter-sweet.

That year, she had been obsessed with the Arthur Ransome books and had persuaded her father to hire a boat so that they could explore the lake in search of the tiny islands where those fictional children had camped fifty years before. Far out on the lake now was a small dinghy, sailed perhaps by other children on that same quest. All at once, terrifyingly, she felt as though she were back in that boat, but this time utterly helpless and alone, with no charts to guide her, no oars, no rudder—and circling around her, silently, remorselessly, a sleek, lethal, grey-eyed shark . . .

'Has madam finished?'

'What? Oh, almost.' And she hastily scooped up a few spoonfuls of avocado.

'You're back, then, Mellie?' Ran was regarding her thoughtfully. 'You look as if you've been a million miles away.'

She eyed him coldly. 'I was merely contemplating my life over the next fifty years or so—and with no great pleasure, either.'

'Really? You do surprise me.' He was baiting her, she knew that, but she was able to ignore the open challenge in his voice, giving her attention instead to the fillet of salmon, wrapped in wafer-thin pastry, which had been placed before her, as he continued, 'A new marriage, a lovely home,' his eyes gleamed, 'a husband whom many other women would give their eye-teeth to have——'

'Just *many* women? Why not say every other woman and be done with it?' She pitched her voice low, so that she was almost hissing across the table at him, and viciously speared a slice of salmon with her fork. 'But of course, they don't know you as I do, do they?'

And yet it was perfectly true what he'd said. She'd been trying, not altogether successfully, to ignore the looks, covert and in some cases quite blatant, that Ran—her *husband*—had been attracting ever since they had entered the room. She slid a glance at him, apparently engrossed again in his meal. He had changed from the formal wedding clothes into casual cream trousers and a black shirt. The grey, well-cut suit had just about contained him in a civilised mould, giving him a veneer of smooth respectability, but now, loosed from the confines of immaculate

London tailoring, he looked once again his old—his *real* lethal self.

No wonder every other woman in the room was feeding on him with at least as much avidity as they were giving to their food! The aura of power, animal drive and energy compounded with his physical good looks to produce a magnetic sexuality so potent that it almost hung in the air around him, like that musky, spicy aftershave he always used.

One woman in particular, an attractive redhead at the next table, was blatantly giving him the come-hither over her companion's unsuspecting shoulder. You poor fool, Mellie wanted to sneer, you've no idea—he'd make mincemeat of you, just as he has me, and every other woman unfortunate enough to cross his path, and enjoy every second of it!

Despite her still simmering anger, Mellie, who in that happier far-off time had so often been in tune with Ran's hiddenmost thoughts, was certain that he was fully aware of the woman's gaze. But he was showing no sign. Instead, he was looking down, toying with the stem of his wine-glass, his lowered eyelids pale and blue-veined between the level black brows and sweep of long black lashes.

Ran . . . As she stared at him, a tight pain suddenly seized her by the throat and to her horror she realised that her eyes were filling with tears. At that moment, as though sensing her eyes on him, he raised his and she hastily looked away. A long moment's silence hung between them, then,

'Dessert?'

'What? Oh, no, thank you.'

'Coffee? Brandy?' His voice was clipped.

'No, thank you.' They would surely choke her.

He raised his finger to summon the waiter and Mellie sat in silence while he settled the bill, her fingers fidgeting endlessly with the metal clasp of her bag. Then, as he stood up, she got jerkily to her feet and followed him from the room.

CHAPTER SEVEN

THE narrow winding road petered out at last into a grassy track. In the deeply banked lanes, they had temporarily lost sight of the mountain peaks, but now they were towering over them again.

They rounded a bend and Ran drew up. Just ahead of them was an open area of roughly mown grass, a stream tumbling through it out towards a small lake, beyond which the grey-green fells rose steeply. At the far end of the lawn was a Swedish-type log cabin, a huge triangle of golden wood against the trees behind, its long windows glinting in the last flame-coloured rays of the sun.

Ran got out and lifted the cases from the boot and she followed him more slowly, her eyes roaming about apprenhensively. The mountains, the lake, the cabin, the wind sighing gently—and nothing else. The whole world had suddenly receded to a thousand miles away.

'What's the matter, Mellie?' There was a cat-like quality about the way he was watching her.

'We're staying *here*?'

He nodded. 'It's mine, my bolt-hole—no telephone, no fax machines, no hassle. I saw it when I was on a climbing holiday a couple of years ago and bought it the same day.'

Mellie stared at him. 'Do you always act

so—precipitately?'

'Not always, no.' He gave her a level look. 'Sometimes I lay my plans well in advance.'

He slung a big black sheepskin-lined canvas coat casually over one shoulder and picked up her case. As he did so, she caught his eye. He was daring her, she just knew, daring her to protest that she wasn't staying here, that she demanded to be taken to a hotel. What was wrong with the one they'd just left, with its lights, cheerful conversations, people—security? She was not alone here—Ran was no more than a yard away from her—but all at once she had an overwhelming, frightening sense of aloneness.

And yet, in other circumstances, this beautiful, isolated spot would make an absolutely perfect setting for a honeymoon . . . Other circumstances . . . other honeymoons . . .

Her lips tightly buttoned against the bleak emptiness that was threatening to take hold of her, Mellie took the overnight bag he was holding out to her and followed him without a word across the single plank which served as a bridge over the narrow stream.

Ran dug out a key from his pocket and opened the door, which led directly into the kitchen, fitted with pale oak units. He dumped the cases and went on through another door, Mellie trailing unwillingly after him. The sitting-room ran the full width of the cabin, the entire front wall taken up with a massive picture window. The whole room was obviously intended to form a backdrop for that superb view, its modern pine furniture, the polished wood floor, the

shades of beige, muted terracotta and olive-green in
the rugs and upholstery giving it a cool, neutral look.

Outside, the mountains were sombre against the
evening sky . . . Mellie shivered suddenly, though
not with cold, and dropped down into the nearest
armchair.

Someone must have earlier switched on the
background central heating, but Ran went over to the
stone fireplace. She watched him cross the room, as
though in slow motion, kneel down and put a match
to the log fire that was laid. Then, as the first yellow
flames leapt sizzling from the dry wood, something
clicked in her brain.

An eternity—four nights ago—he had knelt by the
gas fire in his apartment to perform the same action,
just moments before, armed already with the special
licence, he had finally sprung the trap to which
everything since their first meeting had been leading.
It had all been so carefully, so ruthlessly planned in
sequence, like a dance, this ritual that he had been
enacting with her. All of them—Denis, Chris, Aunt
Livy, but most of all, of course, she herself—all of
them had danced unwittingly to his tune.

She was jerked out of her reverie as he straightened
up, turned to look at her, then took a deliberate step
towards her. She leapt to her feet.

'Keep away from me!'

As he halted, frowning, she went on, 'I mean it,
Ran. Don't you dare touch me.' The slow fuse of
resentment had finally burned through—his arrogant
self-assurance, coupled with her own mingled fear of
his power over her and her anger at her own frailty,
had at last ignited the tinderbox of her fury. 'I

suppose you thought you'd got away with it!'

His eyes narrowed. 'And just what the hell do you mean by that?'

'You know very well what I mean!' As his dark brows jack-knifed down, she hurried on, determined not to allow herself to be intimidated this time. 'You were taking quite a risk, weren't you? If Aunt Livy hadn't been delayed last night, I'd have found out in time and called the whole thing off.'

She gave a short, bitter laugh. 'They say the devil looks after his own—but maybe you didn't need Big Brother's help. You've organised everything else—you probably organised Arnold's petrol pump packing up too!'

It was Ran's turn to laugh. 'Oh, darling, you flatter me. I'm afraid I'm not that ingenious.'

'Really? Don't sell yourself short, Ran. You're the most devious, twisting——'

'Anyway, there was no need for that. You remember we arranged that I should ring your aunt to tell her our joyful news? Well, she was more than happy to go along with my idea that she shouldn't tell you about her plans until our big day. She thought it was a great joke—our little secret, was how she put it, I think.'

'You—you——' Mellie was almost speechless with impotent fury.

'Yes,' Ran went on reminiscently, 'I seem to remember saying—what was it?—something to the effect that the surprise would make your wedding day complete.'

'The only thing needed to make this particular wedding day complete,' she snarled at him, 'would be for you to drop dead in front of me this instant!'

'Sorry to disappoint you, honey.' The light was fading rapidly and his face was a pale blur, except for a pair of gleaming eyes. 'But I don't intend to accommodate you that far—at least, not if I can help it. What was it you said earlier—something about the next fifty years? I'm aiming to——'

'Fifty years? I wouldn't be too sure of that if I were——'

'—to enjoy your company, get to know you, for a long, long time, Mellie. After all, I've waited long enough for that particular pleasure.'

His voice was a sensual, throaty purr and she knew that he was quite deliberately using those innocent-sounding sentiments, those words—know, enjoy, pleasure—in their archaic, original meanings. She felt what little colour she had ebb from her cheeks.

'You're not—I——' she began, then broke off and, in an attempt to regain the initiative, completely changed tack. 'I suppose this was why you were in such a hurry. You knew you wouldn't be able to keep the truth from me for more than a few days. I was even simpleton enough to think, just for a moment, that in spite of everything you said,' her voice was still showing a disturbing tendency to shake, 'it just might have been something else——'

'Yes, you really are a simpleton,' Ran interrupted brusquely. 'I must say I could hardly believe it myself, that you were falling for it. How could you ever have imagined that I could turn Olivia out on to the streets just like that——'

'Very easily. After all, it would have been so much in——'

'—when she's been a sitting tenant for over twenty years.'

Someone was very slowly strangling her. 'You—mean—you—couldn't?'

Ran's complacent laugh rasped on her mind like an emery board. 'Of course not! I couldn't have done it, even if I'd wanted to, and anyway, I had no intention of turning her out. Although, of course, her news did fall rather neatly in with my plans.'

Fall in with his plans . . . No, it was not Aunt Livy but she who, all along the line, had fallen—not neatly but gullibly, credulously—in with his plans.

'I made it all so very easy for you, didn't I?' she said at last, her voice dulled of emotion.

'Like taking candy from a baby,' he agreed gravely, but she could still glimpse that malicious gleam in his eyes, hear that flick of laughter in his voice.

'How you must despise me, though not half as much as I despise myself.'

'No, I don't despise you, Mellie.'

Was there, just for a second, a softer note? But one look at his hard, shadowed face, and she decided not. Her shoulders sagged; fighting Ran was like hurling oneself against a granite cliff, and just about as profitable. He had all but beaten her. Earlier, she had longed for this confrontation—now, weary and dispirited, she didn't even want to be in the same room with him. But at least there was still one way left—just one way for her to assert herself.

Abruptly she gathered up her bag. 'I'm tired. Perhaps you'd show me where my bedroom is?'

'But of course.' Ran was instantly the polite host.

He led her back to the kitchen, picked up her cases,

and went on up the open-tread staircase. A
bathroom, then, under the dormer eaves, a bedroom,
also stretching the width of the house, and, like the
room below, furnished to give an impression of
uncluttered space—a wall of wardrobes, with a fitted
dressing-table, several fringed Indian rugs, and, in
the centre of the room, arranged so that its owner
would have a breathtaking view every morning
through the wall-to-wall window, a large double bed.

Mellie was still eyeing the bed when Ran dumped
her case and bag on the floor, then flicked on wall
lights. 'I didn't bother with curtains—there's nothing
out there apart from the occasional fox.' His eyes met
hers for an instant, but then he added blandly, 'Help
yourself to the bathroom.'

'Th-thank you,' she said breathlessly.

'My pleasure.' He turned away, then stopped as
she mumbled something. 'Yes?' He raised one
eyebrow enquiringly.

'Well—I was just going to say,' her voice was
infuriatingly tight, 'do you want me to help you with
your bed?'

'My—bed?' he repeated slowly.

'Yes, the one downstairs.'

Her parents had an identical, large upholstered
sofa, and she knew it unfolded into a spare bed.

'Thank you, but I can manage perfectly well.'

He had almost closed the door, before she managed
to say, 'Well, goodnight,' but he had gone. As his
footsteps sounded on the stairs, she realised that she
was holding her breath, and now she expelled it in a
slow gust of relief. She had been clenching her hands
in her pockets so tightly that the nails were cutting

through the skin; she drew them out, feeling the tension ebb from her taut muscles.

She snatched up her case and laid it on the cream bedspread. To try and banish the nervous apprehension which was still bubbling away inside her, very slowly and methodically she took out her toilet case, her brush and comb, her nightdress, and laid them in a neat row.

What was Ran doing now? On tiptoe, she crept to the top of the stairs and stood listening, her ears straining for any sound, but none came.

Although she could hardly believe it, he really had gone, and without the slightest demur. Perhaps through some slight feeling of remorse for the way he had deceived her, or even some residue of decency that she would never have credited him with, he had given way on this, at least . . . A dark shadow slanted crookedly across the bottom stair, and Mellie fled to the bathroom.

Once back in the bedroom, she knew instinctively she would not sleep, so she turned off the light and carried the dressing-table stool across to the window. It was dark now, points of moonlight illuminating the slight ripples on the lake and, behind, the hills were black cardboard cut-outs against a few pale stars. A serene, utterly timeless scene, that had not changed for thousands of years and which would remain aeons after their own puny tragedy was turned to ashes in the grave . . .

Mellie gave a wry smile. Philosophy on her wedding night! But what did it matter? Did anything matter beyond the fact that Ran did not love her? She shivered, then realised that she was hugging herself as though she were cold. She got up and, in a vain attempt to banish the shadows which lay within herself far more than in the room, switched on the bedside light.

She took off her blue cotton wrap, then caught sight of her reflection in the mirror. She had resolutely refused to buy any new lingerie for the honeymoon, but she had always loved a small touch of luxury about her, and one of the cheapest ways to indulge this was with pretty undies. Consequently, all her nightdresses were silky slivers, which would reveal far too much creamy pale flesh if Ran just should happen to come back. She looked down at the high-split hemline and the lace inset, which barely concealed her breasts, and swallowed nervously. Suppose he did come in now, this instant? It was desperately important, all of a sudden, that he didn't see her like this.

Hastily she opened her case, turning the contents upside down in her frantic search, then drew out one of the new beach cover-ups in cotton voile which she had bought for those non-existent poolside lunches. High neck, sleeves, a loose, floaty skirt—perfect. She put a hand on the hem of her nightdress, then saw herself reflected in the uncurtained window. Just in case there *was* a fox on the prowl outside, she dropped to her knees beside the bed and, quickly stripping off the nightdress, pulled the beach dress down over her head.

In her trembling haste, though, one of the tiny pearl buttons caught on the fine gold chain she always wore. With an irritable exclamation, she was about to wrench it free, when a pair of strong hands lifted her fingers out of the way.

'Allow me,' Ran's silky voice breathed in her ear.

Mellie, almost smothered in the enveloping folds, froze rigid as she felt the button being released.

'Thanks,' she mumbled, but then, as she felt him lifting the dress clear from her, she clutched at it desperately. 'No! I was just getting into it.'

'Oh, so sorry.' His voice was smooth as Irish cream, but she was not fooled for an instant—he'd known very well what she was doing. With a frisson of terror, she realised that once again she had completely misread Ran. He most definitely had not the slightest intention of meekly retreating to the sofa-bed downstairs.

She snatched the cover-up from him and, still kneeling, scrambled it on anyhow, all the while aware of his eyes lingering over her, so that she could almost feel his gaze scorching her already burning skin. With shaking fingers, her head bent, she did up the buttons, right to the neck.

She could not look up, but was all too conscious of him towering over her, and horrified, she realised that his legs, only inches from her, were bare. Her eyes jerked upwards now to take in the fact that he was wearing the white towelling robe which had been hanging on the bathroom door and she realised that, beneath it, he must be naked.

Ran had not moved, but she could sense the power of his personality reaching out to her, threatening to overwhelm her own faltering will. Desperate to at least free herself from the pose of submissive slave kneeling before her master, she got awkwardly to her feet.

'Don't you ever knock?' Quite unable to meet whatever expression might be in his eyes, she scowled at the brown V of chest.

'Not usually in my own house,' he replied laconically, 'and never at my own bedroom door.'

'*Your* bedroom? I thought I'd made it clear that——'

'Oh, you did—crystal-clear. But I'm afraid that a night spent on a sofa-bed—alone—is not my idea of the ideal wedding night.'

His voice was scarcely above a purr, but Mellie was suddenly very frightened. Somehow, though, she managed to jut her chin and return his challenging gaze.

'You just haven't got the message, have you? You may, thanks to your low-down cunning, have won every round so far, but you're not winning this one. You can get out of my room—now!'

'Oh, no, Mellie.' He smiled, but the hard planes of his face did not soften one iota.

'W-what do you mean?' she whispered.

'I mean that I haven't won every round of the game, as you put it, to be cheated at the final throw by you, my darling.'

She ran her tongue around her dry lips. Quite useless to scream and rave—her only hope of salvation was to keep a cool head. 'Look,' she began, 'I agreed to marry you—I have married you—but I did not say that I'd be y-your wife.'

Ran eyed her thoughtfully. 'A nice distinction, Mellie—but one that I'm afraid I simply cannot go along with.'

'But you must—you must! And what does it matter, anyway? You don't l-love me, not at all,' her voice quivered slightly, 'but you've got me, which is what you wanted all along. As far as everybody—the whole outside world is concerned, we're husband and wife, and—' she managed to inject a spurious defiance, 'you'll have to be satisfied with that.'

'The outside world? No, tonight concerns no one except us two, Lissy.'

Lissy! The old, childish name, which only he had ever used. For an instant the years rolled away, and as she stared at him, huge-eyed, he reached for her and, gently but inexorably, pulled her, unresisting to him.

'Lissy.' His face was buried in her hair and, still holding her tightly, he put up one hand to run his fingers through her black curls. 'Honey-sweet, desirable Lissy. If you knew how much I've longed to do this!' His voice was a thunderous whisper in her ear, his mouth warm against her cold skin.

She felt his lips slide slowly to hers, soft but infinitely persuasive. His towelling robe had fallen open and the heat from his hard body, still damp from his shower, was striking through her fine cotton dress, making her tremulously aware of the yearnings of her own body. His breath, the feel of his hands on her, the potent male scent of him, his strength against her yielding softness—every trembling nerve, every fibre was being drawn out almost beyond breaking-point.

All protests forgotten, aching now to surrender to

him. Mellie felt him lift her off her feet, then he was
laying her down on the bed. He stood over her for a
moment, looking down at her, a dark intense
expression in his grey eyes. With one swift
movement he loosed the belt of his robe. It fell from
him, and the next moment he was beside her.

'Oh, Lissy!'

His hands were sliding up beneath her dress,
across her thighs and the flat plane of her stomach,
finally to take possession of her soft breasts. His long
fingers, their innate strength masked into gentleness,
were stroking them, slowly, gently, until all the
sensations in her body seemed drawn, quivering,
towards them. Through the thin fabric she felt his lips
close on one taut, pulsating centre, and then his
tongue was circling it in an almost unbearably slow,
erotic caress.

At last he raised his head and looked down at her.
His face was flushed, his eyes brilliant, and he smiled
at her as though inviting her to share his sensual
pleasure, the fulfilment of his desire——

Desire. But no tenderness, no love! And the man
above her was not the unskilled, urgent young lad of
eight years before, whom she herself had virtually
seduced. Here was a skilled practitioner in the arts of
sexual love—even down to his deliberate use of her
old pet name—engaged now in seducing her. Mellie's
eyes opened wide. Yes—seducing. And he had all but
succeeded.

But suddenly she knew that she must not let him
succeed. Now, more than ever, she saw just how
vulnerable she was, how fatally simple it would be to
fall once more under Ran's potent spell. It would be

so easy to surrender, to float away on the roaring tide
of his passion. But he did not love her, and she must
not allow herself to love him. Through her own
instinctive response, she had let things go so far that
nothing now would stop him, but while he could
conquer her body, he must not capture her mind, her
heart.

Somehow she forced herself to lie completely
passive as he moved over her, and even when she
sensed the new, driving urgency within him, she
willed herself not to respond, crushing with a
supreme effort of will her answering leap of desire.
Her thighs were being eased apart, but her body did
not open willingly to him, and as she felt him enter
her she bit her lip fiercely to fight back the
unexpected shaft of pain.

Ran's breath rasped, his whole frame was racked
by one final shudder, he gave a long, wrenching
sigh and collapsed on her inert body, totally
spent.

For some moments he lay quite still, but at last he
raised himself to look down at her sombrely. 'Sorry.
You're just too desirable, I guess.' He gave her a
shaky, almost shamefaced smile, that added another
racking twist to her pain. 'But next time it will be
better for you—for both of us, I promise.'

He went to brush her cheek with the side of his
hand, but she jerked away from him. If she let him
touch her now, she would be lost, all her willpower
gone in an instant. 'No, Ran, it won't,' she said
fiercely. 'Oh, there'll be a next time, I know that,
but it won't be any better—not for me, and not for
you.'

'Yes, it will, Mellie. You know you want me as much as I want you. Well,' he smiled wryly at her, 'maybe not quite as much, but you will—I'll make sure of that. I want to feel your lovely body melting in my arms, so that——'

'Oh, yes, that really would flatter your male ego, wouldn't it?' His lips thinned threateningly now, but she smothered the tremor within her. 'But it's not going to be like that. This is the only way it will ever be—cold, mechanical, with not one jot of true feeling in it. It may be called making love, but there'll be nothing of real love, not for either of us.' Her voice was trembling again, but she forced herself to go on. 'And after all, that's only right, isn't it. Ran, in a marriage as loveless as ours?'

His face was shadowed in the moonlight, but she saw, with a blend of bitter satisfaction and fear, that her words had brought an angry flush to his high cheekbones.

'Oh, come now, Mellie, don't let's get sentimental. You're forgetting that I told you before I married you that love means nothing to me. But that doesn't mean that we can't be good for each other, and whatever you may say, I know that you can't hold out against the feelings of your own body.'

'But that's just where you're wrong, Ran. I can.' And she could—a feeling of exultation was sweeping through her—she'd just proved that to herself. 'And in any case, my body is the least part of me. Oh, yes, you can take that whenever you choose—you're so much stronger than me—but it will always be a hollow victory. You'll have nothing that's really me—not my spirit, not my soul, not my love.'

The final words seemed to be torn from her with a savage, pincer-like wrench, and Mellie knew that weak, desolate tears were threateningly close, but then, to her infinite relief, Ran shrugged.

'You're a sentimental fool, Mellie, but if that's the way you feel, OK. And don't worry,' his lips curled into a twisted smile, 'about me—taking you, I mean. I've never taken a woman by force yet, and I don't intend making a start with my own wife. No, the next move in that direction is down to you. But I'll just tell you this, sweetie,' his voice was basalt-hard now, 'whatever your plans may be, for the next fifty years or so, I certainly do not intend staying celibate for the rest of my life!'

His words stunned her into silence and as she looked at him, hot tears pricking now at her eyes, he lifted himself from the bed, then opened the covers at the far side and slid under them.

'W-what are you doing?' she asked.

'Getting into bed, of course. And if you're thinking of sleeping on that sofa-bed, forget it. The door's locked.'

With that, he turned on his side, and immediately appeared to relax effortlessly into sleep. Mellie lay, propped on her elbow, watching him, his head dark against the cream pillow, his black lashes shadowing the hard grey eyes, a maelstrom of tangled emotions churning within her. She tried to rekindle her anger, to hug this to her, but an utter, numbing weariness was now advancing inexorably through her whole body so that at last, very carefully, she too drew back the covers to slip between the cool sheets.

Countless hours later, she descended into a dark, comfortless oblivion.

CHAPTER EIGHT

WHEN Mellie woke the next morning, the bed beside her was empty, and when she put a hand to the indentation in the pillow where Ran's head had lain it was quite cold.

Her eyes strayed to the window and just for a moment the image came to her of how it might have been. Of waking, entwined in each other's arms, to gaze out at that glorious view, she warm, alive, fulfilled. She had so often dreamed of this, but now, in the reality, the dream had turned to nightmare . . .

Somehow she forced herself out of bed and showered. What to wear? Although the sun was shining, there was a distinct chill in the air and, riffling through the lightweight cottons and linens, she drew out a pair of baggy lemon cotton trousers and a white crochet sweater which she had included in case the tropical evenings turned cool. Well, they would have to do.

She was just sliding the wardrobe doors to when in the far corner something glinted, catching her eye. She leaned in and retrieved the object, then straightened. Looking down at the beautiful sapphire and diamond gold earring which lay in her palm, she was totally unprepared for the stab of sick pain, as though a knife had struck, then twisted in her vitals.

She stared at it for what seemed a long time, then

dressed and went slowly downstairs to the kitchen, where Ran, in black tracksuit and trainers, was grilling bacon, mushrooms and tomatoes. Ignoring her queasy protests, he placed a piled-up plate in front of her.

'Get on the outside of that—I'm taking you into Keswick this morning.' His voice was brisk and impersonal, and she was grateful for this, at least.

She pushed a tomato round her plate. 'What are we—you planning on doing there?'

'Getting you kitted out. Walking boots, overtrousers, cagoule.'

'Oh, there's absolutely no need.' The tension of being face to face with Ran again, after the trauma of the scene the previous night, was putting a spiked edge into her voice.

'But there is—every need. As you so rightly pointed out, bikinis—however delicious—' she kept her eyes fixed to her plate and gave all her attention to neatly dissecting a mushroom'—are hardly ideal wear for a honeymoon in these parts.'

'Speaking of ideal honeymoon wear,' she dug in the pocket of her trousers, and sent the earring spinning wildly across the table, 'I found this upstairs, in the bedroom,' she said coldly.

Ran trapped it beneath the flat of his hand, picked it up and slid it into his pocket. 'Thanks,' his voice was deadpan, 'Jackie will be relieved—or rather, her insurers will.'

Mellie wouldn't ask—she would not allow herself to ask. 'Right.' She gathered up the plates and shot them into the sink. 'Ready when you are.'

In Keswick she was fitted with soft leather boots,

climbing trousers and several expensive, beautifully warm Lakeland sweaters. She wanted to protest, What's the point? We shall never come here together again. But, in the face of a certain tight line around Ran's mouth, a slight drawing down of the dark brows, the words stayed unsaid.

After that, as though intent on putting her through a brutal training programme for some gruelling marathon, he took her walking and climbing all day and each day, until she was almost tottering with exhaustion. Still, she was glad of the physical exertion and the mind-blowing fatigue which followed it, for it gave her virtually no time to do what she most dreaded—think.

They seemed, by silent mutual consent, to have agreed on an uneasy truce. After that first night, Ran made no further move towards her, and did sleep on the bed downstairs. Alone in the big double bed, her thoughts went round and round like a small animal trapped on a treadmill. What shall I do? How can we go on like this? What had Ran said? 'I certainly do not intend staying celibate for the rest of my life.' How long ago was it that Jackie had lain in this bed? How long would it be before the next redhead crossed his path—and next time, he might not be so unresponsive to the frank invitation in her eyes.

The tension was there, between them, all the time, and Mellie sensed that the slightest move on her part would provoke an answering response from Ran, but she knew, with a fearful certainty, that she could never recreate the iron control of her wedding night when, aching to hold him in her arms, cradle his dark head to her, she had none the less lain completely passive and unresponding. Another time, she would inevitably succumb to the forbidden sweetness, and that would deliver her totally into her husband's unloving power.

Only one afternoon suddenly threatened to be shatteringly different. It was very hot, and after walking high on the fells they had come down to collapse in the shade of some rowan trees beside a still pool. As Mellie leaned back, her bare arm brushed inadvertently against Ran's and she jerked away as though he had burned her. Ran's mouth tightened and he sprang to his feet.

'I'm going to have a go at tickling trout.' He spoke without looking at her, in that clipped, unemotional voice he had taken to using.

Throwing himself full-length on the bank, he lowered one arm into the water. Mellie leaned her head back against one of the tree-trunks, closing her eyes against the sun which dazzled through the leaves. When she opened them, half blinded by the light, Ran was still lying there motionless, almost at her feet. His face was slightly averted and he was frowning in concentration; his chin was propped on his hand, his hair falling over his eyes, shading them so that they looked less cruel—softer, even vulnerable . . .

For Mellie, it was a moment frozen in time, slow and endless. As she stared down at him, a terrible dread—no, more, a sick certainty seized her, its grip almost physical in its potency. Of course. The thought came quite matter-of-factly—I love him. I've never stopped loving him. Then, *Oh, what shall I do?*

'Got him!' shouted Ran.

He turned towards her, grinning in boyish triumph and holding a wriggling brook trout between his fingers. Their eyes met full-on—for the first time in days. Something, flickering and intangible, flashed between them, and the fish dropped back into the water. But as Ran straightened up, Mellie jumped to her feet and began scrambling blindly away through the rocks.

When at last, reluctantly, she slowed her headlong flight, Ran's face as he sauntered up to her wore its habitual cold, shuttered look, wiped clear of all expression.

Back in Keswick, he pulled into a parking space.

'I want to make a phone call. You stay here.'

While he was gone, she resolutely kept her mind occupied with watching the holidaymakers and locals thronging the narrow pavements of the pretty, bustling little town. When Ran at last came back, he threw himself in beside her.

'Something's cropped up. I need to get down to London.' He was already easing the big car out into the flow of traffic. 'I take it you won't object overmuch if we go home tomorrow?'

Mellie winced inwardly at the biting sarcasm. 'Of course not,' she said huskily, looking straight ahead at a group of walkers ambling dangerously across the road just ahead. 'Why on earth should I?'

'. . . and if you'll just take the rest of this junk outside, Mellie, love.' Olivia wiped a grimy hand across her hot face and got up from her knees with a groan. 'Really, I'd no idea I'd accumulated such a load of rubbish! I don't think I can have thrown anything away in the last twenty years.' She sighed. 'I'm almost beginning to ask myself if it's all worth it.'

'Now, now, Aunt Livy.' Mellie clicked her tongue teasingly. 'What would Arnold say if he heard you? And besides, you know you can hardly wait for the wedding.'

Her aunt laughed and flushed, so that for an instant Mellie glimpsed the pretty young girl in the middle-aged woman. 'Well, perhaps you're right. And you've been a great help, my pet—I'm so disorganised, I'd never have managed it without you.' She peered at her niece anxiously. 'You're looking really worn out, though—I hope it hasn't been too much for you.'

'Oh, I'm fine, Aunt Livy, honestly.' And seizing the cardboard box of kitchen cupboard rubbish, Mellie fled.

When she returned, though, her aunt was clearly not ready to let the subject drop. 'You do look very pale, love. Are you sure you're all right?' She shot her a disconcertingly perceptive glance.

'Of course I am. I—I expect it's the heat, getting me down a bit.'

'Hmm.' Olivia sounded unconvinced. 'I just wonder if you're doing too much. You've been working really hard the last few weeks, ever since you came back from your honeymoon. I know you enjoy your work at the Manor, but I'm sure Ran would be happier for you to give up——'

'And do what?' Mellie bit her lip sharply on the jagged edge in her voice, and turned away hastily to yet another overflowing cupboard.

'And just be his wife,' Olivia said drily. As her niece's busy hands stilled for a moment, she went on, 'Of course, that's old-fashioned, I know—heresy coming from a woman like me who's done her own thing all her life. But—well, Ran is——'

'Ran,' Mellie put in smoothly, and shot a handful of empty bottles into the box. 'And he doesn't mind, not at all, me doing my own thing, as you call it.' In fact, not only does he not mind, he doesn't care whether I work until I drop—not that he seems to know whether I'm even there——

'It's nothing to do with me, and you can tell me to mind my own business if you like, but I know Ran—I've known him since he was a little boy—and even though he seems so self-sufficient, so independent, I'm sure that underneath he's no different from any other man, and he needs the security of a stable home, a loving wife.'

Oh, but you're wrong, so totally wrong. Ran doesn't need anything—at least, not from me . . . Mellie dragged the final few empty bottles to the front of the shelf and began loading them into the box with such violence that several cracked.

'Finished. Oh no, there's one more.' She pulled out the small, dusty bottle, a brackish-looking liquid slopping around inside it. 'I don't suppose you want this?'

Her aunt took the bottle, frowning down at it. 'Good heavens, I'd forgotten all about this.' She gave a laugh. 'My patent aphrodisiac!'

As Mellie stared up at her, she went on, rather shamefacedly, 'You remember those talks I used to give to women's groups and so on, about herbalism?

Well, I used to touch on plants that were used as love potions, and—as a joke really—I made one up from a 'receipt' in an old herbal. It was amazing how many young—and not so young—women would ring me up or come and see me, and beg me for some. Of course, it was never for them—it was always for their best friend or their sister.' Olivia sighed. 'You know, love, there must be an awful lot of unhappiness around that we just don't know about.'

Mellie bit down a wild, crazy desire to jump up, laughing hysterically, then collapse in floods of tears against her aunt's filthy overall. 'Yes, I'm sure there is,' she said woodenly.

'Of course, all the ingredients were quite harmless—savory, borage, southernwood, that sort of thing. None of your eyes of newts and toes of frogs, but the amazing thing is, it seemed to work. I had quite a reputation at one time—the white witch of Stanton Morville!'

She broke off with a reminiscent smile and tossed the bottle on to the pile. 'It's a long time ago now. Throw them all away while I make a cup of tea, then I'll show you my wedding suit. I do hope it isn't too young for me.'

'Dear Aunt Livy, how I'm going to miss you!' Mellie hugged her convulsively and her voice trembled ever so slightly. 'I'm sure it isn't—you're going to look absolutely wonderful!'

And she certainly did, Mellie thought. Standing beside Ran, so heartachingly handsome and so close in the church pew that their sleeves brushed, she had seen a kind of glowing radiance in Olivia's face that surely, six weeks earlier, had been all too lacking in herself . . .

'Sorry to disturb you, madam.'

Mellie jumped at the sound of the housekeeper's voice just behind her and guiltily picked up the pen which had lain untouched for half an hour, the letter to her parents describing the wedding still not started.

'You'll remember I've promised to babysit for our Jenny tonight—they're going to the Midsummer Eve dance in the village hall. So, if you don't mind, I'll be getting off as soon as I've served the first course, Mrs Owen.'

Mrs Pearson, who had never once managed 'Miss Grant', was getting her tongue around the new title with remarkable ease, Mellie thought with a twinge of dull resentment. Mrs Owen—the coldly formal name seemed to be isolating her still further from her past life, and she longed to blurt out, 'Please—call me Mellie still', but instead she said, her voice mechanical, 'Yes, of course, Mrs Pearson, go as soon as you like. In fact, I'll serve the meal.'

When the housekeeper had gone, she pushed back her chair and stood up precipitately. The letter would have to wait yet another day. She heard Mrs Pearson going downstairs, then moments later Ran's voice as they met in the old stone-flagged hall below, now beautifully restored. She hadn't set eyes on him all day, but as his footsteps sounded on the bottom stair she fled to the corner spiral staircase.

Half-way up, she heard the telephone ringing in the room she had just left, then Ran answering it. She hovered uncertainly, picking absentmindedly with her thumbnail at a piece of fretted stonework, then went on up.

The spiral staircase led directly through his bedroom. Every time Mellie came up and down stairs, she was forced to pass through it, seeing the massive four-poster in which he slept, the small signs of his occupation—a pair of shoes kicked off, a heap of loose change or keys on the otherwise uncluttered dressing-table.

Once, he had obviously gone out in a hurry, and there was a heap of clothes lying across a chair. Hardly aware of what she was doing, she had gone into the room, hung the trousers up on a hanger in the wardrobe, then picked up the chunky cream Arran sweater, meaning to fold it in a drawer. Instead, though, she had stood, holding it against her for a long time fancying—quite ridiculously, for Ran had been gone at least an hour—that it still retained some of his body warmth. Then she put it away.

She herself slept in one of the smaller rooms on the floor above, which Ran had already equipped as a guest suite. On their return from honeymoon, she had made it quite clear that she intended using this, and Ran had grunted carelessly, 'Suit yourself.' And he had remained in solitary occupation of his king-sized four-poster.

The room's most recent use had obviously been as a nursery, and the window-bars were still in place. It was a pretty, airy room, but as Mellie lay in bed night after night, the moonlight, filtering through the William Morris chintz curtains, cast an elongated shadow of the bars across the soft green carpet, like the criss-cross mesh of a cage . . .

She heard rapid footsteps coming up the stairs and then Ran appeared in the doorway.

'Anything cropped up while I've been out?'

'The landscape architect called. There may be a problem with the golf course—something about subsidence from the old limestone workings.'

'Damn!' He frowned. 'Oh, well, he can sort it out. That's what I'm paying him for.'

They were speaking to each other, Mellie noted dispassionately, in that curious way they had developed—of talking, yet not talking to each other, of looking, yet not looking at each other.

'Was it him on the phone just now?' she heard herself ask.

'No. Something's come up. I'm going to have to fly to the States.'

'When?'

'Tomorrow morning.'

So soon? And no word of regret that he was going, or any hint that she might go with him? Well, she would certainly not ask. But at least, perhaps the dull, throbbing pain which she felt all the time now would ease when a few thousand miles of grey Atlantic lay between them. She moistened her lips.

'And—and how long will you be away?'

She must have just about succeeded in infusing a 'not that I care in the slightest, you understand' note into her voice, for Ran responded instantly to it with an offhand shrug.

'Not sure really. A week or so, I expect.'

He turned away.

'W-would you like me to help you pack?'

He paused on the top stair, then, without turning,

replied, 'No, thanks, I'll do it myself after dinner.'

The chill in his voice made her feel physically cold in spite of the warmth of the June evening and she closed her eyes, listening as he descended to the floor below—to his territory—as for a moment that sick ache became the equally familiar sharp knife-thrust of anguish.

She went to shower and get ready for dinner. In the dressing-table mirror, her face was completely devoid of expression. The sheer intense dreadfulness of the first couple of weeks after their return had been unbearable, as over and over again tears had threatened her fragile composure. Now, though, she had become such an adept at hiding her inner self that even when she was alone, the mask hardly ever slipped.

She stared impassively into the green eyes of that sombre other self in the glass, while the thoughts jangled like a terrible incantation: Ran doesn't love me, doesn't love me, doesn't love me. He never would love her, however much she might secretly, achingly love him. If only she could cross over the years and bring back the past—that magical time when he truly had loved her, had held her among the bluebells and the ferns and called her his little green-eyed witch.

Magical? Witch? Witchcraft? 'I had quite a reputation at one time—the white witch of Stanton Morville' . . .

With the slow deliberateness of a sleepwalker, Mellie got up, went through to the bathroom, opened the cabinet and took out the small bottle. It lay cold in her hand and just for a moment she felt again the potent mix of excitement, fear—and guilt—she had experienced when, unseen by her aunt, her heart beating violently, she had snatched it back out of the bin.

Some force had seized her, was driving her on now. She had already laid out a dress—pale blue linen—on the bed, but she put it back and fetched out instead the only dress that she knew she could wear tonight. Midsummer Eve—a night for magic, for sorcery, for witchcraft.

She slipped it on and saw the pale grey chiffon skirt float softly around her legs, the draped folds of the neckline frame her delicate face and neck like the petals of a flower. She heard Ran going downstairs, hesitated for one moment, then caught up the bottle and, holding it tightly in her palm, followed him down to the sitting-room.

He was bending over his desk, sorting out some papers, and she stood in the doorway for a moment watching him, unseen, but then he must have sensed that she was behind him, for he turned sharply. His eyes took in the dress, her slender body, and just for an instant some expression flickered in them before he deliberately lowered his gaze and turned abruptly back to the desk.

Throughout the meal he was even more silent than usual, as though the Atlantic already lapped between them, but Mellie was hardly aware of his moody preoccupation with the pattern on the linen tablecloth. She only felt the weight of the small bottle which lay concealed in her lap.

At last, though, to distract herself, she said, 'This trip to the States—is it business?'

'Yes.' Ran did not look up from his plate.

'Are you—promoting the Manor over there? Is that why you're going?'

'No.'

There was a forbidding, end-of-conversation quality to the word which all but silenced her, but, swallowing her pride, she forced herself to make one more attempt.

'Can I——?' She stopped.

'Yes?' There was a snap in his voice—he was obviously irritated at being dragged out of his private thoughts again.

She wanted to jump up, bang her fists on the table and scream, Look, can't you understand? I don't want you to leave me, I can't bear for you to be away from me. Let me come with you, *please*, but instead she said quietly, 'If you've finished, I'll make some coffee.'

Alone in the kitchen, she waited for the coffee to percolate, her arms folded across her breasts, the bottle, now sticky with her sweat, still clutched in one hand. It was no use, of course—she knew that already. No aphrodisiac, however potent, was going to work with Ran; he had already withdrawn irretrievably from her, his mind thousands of miles away.

Perhaps this was how it was always going to be. The conference centre would open very soon and Ran—that complex bundle of nervous energy and driving ambition—would not be content to stay here. The Manor was, after all, only one of his many business ventures, and to the outside world it would merely appear that, like any other high-powered businessman, he always needed to be on the move. Only they two would know the truth—that he had constantly and increasingly to distance himself from her.

The coffee-pot began to sputter softly and she poured out two cups. With slightly unsteady hands, she uncorked the tiny bottle, then sniffed at the greenish liquid. No smell, but how would it taste? Would he drink it, and if he did, might it hurt him—*poison* him? . . . 'Members of the jury, you see before you this fiend in female form, this wicked witch . . .' A nervous giggle was bubbling up in her throat; she clasped one hand across her mouth and with the other slurped most of the potion into Ran's cup.

At first, it did not seem as if he was going to drink any of it. When she came back, he was still sitting hunched over the table; he got up and threw himself down into an armchair, scowling at the carpet and flicking the teaspoon against his saucer.

'Y-your coffee's getting cold.'

Mellie could not quite keep the tremor out of her voice, but he did not seem to notice. She watched him covertly over the rim of her cup, veiling her eyes with her lashes whenever she sensed his glance straying towards her.

After an eternity, he finally snatched up his cup and drained it, then resumed his morose inspection of the carpet. Mellie continued to watch him, the spiral of tension building inside her until it was all she could do to sit still, her hands clenched together in her lap. The huge antique grandfather clock struck the half-hour and at last Ran stirred.

'Would you like another cup?' Perhaps if she gave him the rest of the mixture . . .

'No, thanks. It was poisonous stuff.' He grimaced. 'If that's the best you can do, thank heavens Mrs Pearson will be back tomorrow!'

'But you won't be here tomorrow, will you?' The words were out of their own volition.

'That's true.' As though hardly able to get away from her fast enough now, he sprang to his feet. 'I'm going to pack.'

He did not look at her, was already half-way to the door.

'Are you sure I can't help you?' Tentatively Mellie tried again, still hoping, against all appearances, that the meal, if not the potion, had mellowed him slightly, but he merely said brusquely,

'No, thanks.' He paused. 'I shall be gone when you get up—I'll see you when I get back. My New York number will be on the desk in case of any problems.' And he was gone.

Burning tears were blinding her, but she blinked them angrily away. It hadn't worked. Well, of course it hadn't—she'd known that all along. For a moment her face crumpled like a hurt child's, then she got up awkwardly and carried the coffee tray out to the kitchen. She poured the rest of the mixture away, dropped the empty bottle into the bin and returned listlessly to the sitting-room.

The day had been scorching and the evening was hardly any cooler, so that in spite of the open windows the room was filled with oppressive heat. Mellie passed her hand across her eyes in a gesture of intense, bone-breaking weariness. What to do now?

Read? Watch television? *No*—when Ran had finished packing, he might well come back to do some last-minute work at his desk, and she simply couldn't endure that cold, aloof expression again.

Instead, she went downstairs and let herself out, to roam like an automaton around the grounds. The orchard was still overgrown; she walked through the avenues of gnarled, silvery trees, her grey skirt draggling against the long grass; then into the Orangery, where the intoxicating perfume of the white jasmine, trapped by the still heat of the day, made her dizzy. Then finally, with a kind of inevitability, to the maze.

In the unearthly, luminous light, its dark overshadowed mouth had an unnervingly menacing quality. No wonder children always avoided the place, even in daylight—and tonight of all nights! Mellie swallowed, feeling the goosebumps of terror rise on her arms, and began to turn away, but then she stopped. Surely, Midsummer Eve. If there ever was any magic in this place it would be here, this waiting night . . .

She had not come here since that dreadful encounter with Jason, but tonight Jason seemed as distant as one of those white stars overhead. That was the night that Ran had told her about his childhood visit—and *his* dearest wish had been granted . . . He'd brought a dead fieldmouse as his offering—'remember, you must take a present for the witch' . . .

A herbaceous border lay alongside the holly hedge. Mellie picked a few shaggy-headed daisies, their white circles small emblems of the moon, and, her heart now pounding painfully under her ribs, she slipped inside.

The tall hedges had been clipped, but even so the pathways were narrow, claustrophobic, leaves clawing at her bare arms like long-nailed fingers. She had forgotten how small the maze was—and how watchful. It seemed to turn in on itself, holding its secrets. No children would ever want to play hide and seek here; there was an almost tangible, brooding quality to the place. Her mouth was dry with fear and as she came nearer to the centre an almost overwhelming urge seized her to turn and run headlong back.

At the exact moment that she stepped out from intense black shadow into the pale half-light of the small grassy space which lay at the heart of the maze, and where the hedges were clipped into the five-sided shape of a pentangle, a sickle moon slid silently up above the hedge. Mellie took a deep breath, then closed her eyes and let the flowers drop from her icy fingers.

'Please, whoever you are, let him love me,' she whispered. 'Please, let Ran love me!'

She stood with her eyes screwed up, listening—her senses heightened by her absolute aloneness. But there was no sound, not even the sighing of the wind, and at last she opened them. The flowers lay at her feet; she touched one of them gently with the toe of her sandal and the petals fell.

She turned to go, then stood motionless, one hand to her throat. At the far end of the path something white was glimmering; something—a tall, unmistakable figure—was bearing swiftly down on her.

CHAPTER NINE

THE spell had worked. She had called him up, summoned him to her.

Ran halted, the width of the pentangle between them. His features were in shadow, but his eyes were fixed on her face, the same watchful quality in them that she had sensed in the maze itself.

'What the hell are you doing in here?' There was a harsh edge to his voice which made her flinch.

'I——' Her throat was tight.

'You look as though you've seen a ghost. What is it—what's the matter?'

He crossed the space between them in two strides and stood looking down at her intently, his eyes a strange silvery grey in the luminous dusk. Was he real—or was he a ghost, a demonic spirit in the bodily form of Ran, that somehow she had raised? Hardly knowing what she was doing, Mellie put one hand flat against his chest, and beneath the white shirt, felt the warm, totally human solidity of the man.

'Mellie?' Ran's voice was suddenly husky.

He put the side of his hand under her chin and gently raised her face until she was forced to meet his gaze. They stared at each other for endless moments, then he gave a shaky laugh and gathered her into his arms.

'Oh, my sweet Lissy!' One hand was tangling in

her black curls, the other clasped the small of her back, straining her to him, his lips tracing the line of her upturned throat, her chin, her lips. The kiss, gentle at first, quickly deepened into passion, as he slid his tongue into her mouth, moving it around in voluptuous exploration until, closing her eyes, she sagged against him.

'Sweetheart, listen to me.'

Mellie gave a tiny moan of protest, but Ran was holding her away from him, his hands gripping on her elbows almost cruelly, with the intensity of his feeling.

'Listen to me,' he repeated. 'I want every part of you. After what you said—that night——' his voice was ragged, 'I swore I'd never take you, never make love to you, unless you gave me everything of yourself. You told me I'd never have your spirit, your soul, your love.' She flinched at the echo of her exact words. 'Well, I want all of you—or none of you.' He gave her a little shake. 'Do you understand?'

She forced herself to look up. In the dim light she saw his ravaged face, the pain in his eyes, and her heart twisted. She had meant to hurt him, and yet—her proud, inviolate husband almost pleading with her? This anguish she had inflicted on them both had gone on for long enough—she simply couldn't stand out any longer against the depths of his need for her.

Too shy to answer him in words, she smiled softly at him, then, reaching up, slid both hands into his thick hair and gently drew his face down to kiss him. Against her mouth, Ran gave a wholly incoherent exclamation, then began kissing her, the violent, greedy kisses of a famished man, until her lips and mouth throbbed under him.

Still locked so tightly against each other that she could feel his heart pounding against her flesh, they sank to their knees on the soft grass. She felt his hands, slightly unsteady, on her, then he was unzipping her dress, lifting the folds of grey chiffon away from her, then she heard his breath catch harshly in his throat at the sight of her slender body, her bare breasts pearl-like in the soft moonlight.

He held her against him and brushed one finger lightly across each breast, so that they both felt the tingling centres pulsate under the butterfly touch. Then he laid her down, his arms still beneath her, lifting her slightly clear of the ground, first to slide her lace panties off, then to kiss and caress her to such an exquisite pitch of pleasure that it seemed as though she could not bear it any longer, before his lips and hands moved on to a new place, a new throbbing part of her. White-hot flames licked through her and her entire body seemed about to be consumed in this terrifying conflagration which Ran had lit within her.

She tried to pull him down to her, but he resisted, capturing her wrists with one hand, even though at the same time she sensed his iron control begin to fracture. But her craving for him, so long denied, gave her a fierce strength and she tore her hands free and dragged him down towards her again, at the same time fumbling open the buttons on his shirt to slide the palm of one hand across his moist, smooth skin.

The potent male scent of his body was all around her, on her, so that she felt drunk on it. The brass buckle of his trousers defeated her and Ran would not help her, so she slipped her small hands down inside the waistband to rest them, fingers splayed against the taut line of his buttocks, her thumbs softly caressing the small, secret indentations at the base of his spine.

She felt him shudder under her insistent touch, then he dragged her hands clear and stood up, peeling his trousers down over his slim, tightly muscled hips and thighs. She bit her lip at the power of his body—and at the knowledge of the power she had over that body—then, as he came down towards her again, she moved her head away, closing her eyes to go into the darkness of her own body's blazing desire.

But Ran turned her head back to him. 'Look at me, Mellie,' he whispered. 'I want to see your eyes—I want you to see me.'

Obediently, she opened her eyes, then as he at last entered her she arched to receive him, offering herself to him, taking him into her in total loving acceptance. He possessed her with a raw urgency that made her cry out with the intense joy that was almost a sweet pain, and she put her arms around him, clasping him even more tightly to her, so that she could hear his breath thundering in her ears.

Drowning in passion, she moved in unison with him, then finally, as the million ecstatic sensations in her all fused to that quivering central point of her being, she bit back a long cry against Ran's shoulder

as, simultaneously, the tidal wave snatched them up
and dashed them down, with one long, shuddering
spasm of ecstatic joy, to lie spent in each other's
arms . . .

At last Ran raised his head and smiled down at her,
a tight, lopsided little smile, then gently brushed the
damp hair from her brow. When she lifted her hand
to stroke his cheek, he seized it, pressing his lips into
the moist palm.

'Beautiful Mellie,' he murmured against her skin,
'beautiful, bewitching Mellie!'

Bewitching! Oh, heavens—she'd really succeeded!
Whether it was the potion or her plea in the maze,
she'd put a spell on him!

He must have felt the faint tremor that ran through
her, for he said, 'What's wrong?'

'Well——' she began guiltily. 'Oh, nothing.'

'Yes, there is. What's the matter?'

'Well—' she broke off, then unwillingly, 'it's just
that I stole some of Aunt Livy's home-made
aphrodisiac. I—I put it in your coffee.'

'So that's why it tasted like stagnant drainwater!'
He shook her again, impatiently this time. 'Oh, you
fool, Mellie—you absolute little fool!'

He was angry with her. She shouldn't have told
him. 'Yes, I'm sorry. It was just that—there didn't
seem to be any other way to——' Her voice tailed
off.

'Don't you know, Mellie, that your body's the
only aphrodisiac I need? Never mind any of Olivia's
rat poison, it's you, just you, that's bewitched
me.'

Yes, but suddenly that wasn't enough—nothing

like enough. But wasn't this how it was always going to be: her aching, trembling love finely balanced against, utterly dependent on, his physical desire?

'I suppose that's why you looked so shifty just now. A guilty conscience at having nearly polished off your husband!' Ran tapped the end of her nose in mock admonition.

'Not exactly.' She tried to look back at him steadily. 'You see, it didn't seem to have worked, so I—I asked the witch to make you love me. Oh, it doesn't matter, really,' as she saw his lips twist. She gave him a faintly sad smile. 'I love you—what was it you said?—body and soul—and I always will. It's no use trying to hide it any longer, and that's enough for me. So——'

He put two fingers softly across her lips to silence her. 'Mellie.' The pause was a long one. 'Mellie, I lived so long without love that I don't even know whether I understand what that word means. But if loving someone is having an ache in my guts all the time, of hardly being able to bear her out of my sight, of wanting her with me as long as I live, then—I love you.' He gave her a crooked smile. 'Will that do?'

He was giving her the whole world and asking her if it was enough. 'Oh, yes.' Somehow she must lighten his sombre mood. She caught his hand and kissed it gently. 'I think that'll do.'

There was one question, though, that she had to ask. 'Ran,' she murmured against his palm, 'why did you feel that you had to trick—blackmail me into marrying you?'

He blew out his breath pensively. 'Because, my

darling, I wasn't in the least sure that you loved me still. After all, you'd given precious little sign of it. And besides, you'd always been so much under the influence of your father that I was terrified that, given half a chance, he'd snatch you from me again. I was determined that, this time, I wasn't going to lose you to him—or any other man.'

Conscious perhaps of the vehemence of his tone, he gave her a wry smile. 'Of course, for a man who's always prided himself on managing very nicely on his own, loving you the way I do is not a very comfortable sensation to live with. Apart from anything else, I could hit any man you even look at, kill any man you smile at.'

Mellie flinched at the violence in his voice. 'But, Ran, there's no need, no need at all. Do you think I've even looked at another man, much less fallen for one?' There was still a frightening hardness in his eyes, but she managed to force a gently teasing smile. 'You see, I fell in love with this guy when I was fifteen, and—well, he spoilt me for anybody else.'

He regarded her for long moments, his face taut, then to her intense relief she sensed him relax. He smiled, then in one fluid movement he got to his feet, drawing her up with him.

He was helping her into her dress when she caught sight of his shoulder. The smooth, tanned skin was defaced by a distinct double row of teeth marks, from the corner of which a tiny trickle of blood had oozed, then congealed. She clapped her hand to her mouth.

'Oh, no! I'm sorry.'

'Think nothing of it.' He gave her a meaning look, and just for a moment the colour rushed to her face as she remembered her untrammelled ecstasy in their lovemaking.

Just as they were leaving, Mellie caught sight of the flowers, still lying where she had dropped them. She stooped and picked them up, but they were already wilting, crushed beneath their two bodies, so she let them fall again. A present for the witch . . .

At the front door of the Manor, Ran scooped her up into his arms and carried her up the winding stone stairway into his bedroom. Still holding her, he smiled down at her, a warmth and tenderness in his grey eyes that she had never seen before.

'It is—all right now, isn't it, Ran?' she asked tremulously, as he gently laid her down on the huge four-poster bed.

'Perfectly.' He kissed her. 'Perfectly.' He kissed her again, then drew the pale blue embossed silk hangings around the bed, so that they were at once cocooned in a warm, utterly private world. 'All right, for ever, darling Lissy.'

When Mellie finally awoke next morning Ran had already gone, but strangely she felt no sadness. The smell, the touch of his body, was still on hers, and she was filled with a languorous, dreamy sweetness. Clasped in his arms, she had been all but engulfed in the fierce tide of his possessive love as he began to teach her the secrets of her body, and his own, until she had gloried in her power to rouse him, draw him to the heights and then join him there.

She yawned and stretched luxuriously like a replete

tigress, seeing the faint bruises, like the dusky skin of
grapes, on her arms and breasts, then turned towards
Ran's side of the bed. Lying in the exact centre of the
pillow was one shaggy-headed daisy. He must have
crept out and picked it, then tiptoed back upstairs to
place it there. Beside it lay a hastily torn piece of
notepaper, on which he had scribbled, 'An offering
for my own little witch'.

Mellie picked up the flower and saw, lying on the
pure white petals, a huge bead of dew. It rolled off,
glistening for a moment in the air, then fell on to
her bare midriff. Exactly like a tear—she stared down
at it as a strange sensation, almost of fear, an echo of
her feelings in the maze the previous night, trick-
led unnervingly down her spine, then, smiling at
her own superstitious imaginings, she flicked it
away.

For the next two days, however, Mellie found it
almost impossible to settle to anything. There was
plenty, really, that could have occupied her time to
overflowing—the kitchen staff were due to join them
in just over two weeks and she wanted to be sure that
everything was ready for them—but instead she
found herself fidgeting around the house, getting in
everyone's way, as her thoughts constantly strayed.
Where was he . . . what was he doing now, at this
precise moment?

Ran had not told her any more of why he had so
suddenly had to make this trip—only to say that he
really did have to go but would be back just as soon
as he could manage it. He had rung her the last two
evenings from his hotel, but the sound of his voice,

so amazingly clear, had only served to increase the longing she felt for him to be back with her. What had he said last night, just before he rang off? She blushed scarlet at the memory, and determinedly set to work again.

On the morning of the third day, she had abandoned the futile struggle to fix her mind on a series of alternative wholefood menus she had been provisionally devising for the more determined—or desperate—guests, and gone for a long walk in the grounds. When she at last returned, Mrs Pearson met her in the entrance hall.

'Oh, you've just missed Mrs Bennett. She was sorry you were out.'

Mellie guiltily suppressed a sigh of relief. The vicar's wife, the most well-meaning of women, was capable of talking for hours, once started, and she had already lost enough time this morning.

'Did she want anything in particular, Mrs Pearson?'

'Well, apparently they're already planning ahead for Christmas and they were wondering if they could hold the children's Sunday School party at the Manor. It always was held here, of course, in the old days, before Sir Ranulf's time, of course.'

Before Sir Ranulf's time—yet another of the village traditions that he had summarily put a stop to. Mellie remembered her mother and Aunt Livy fondly recollecting long-ago festivities at the Manor and she smiled with pleasure, picturing a huge tree in the main hall . . . fairy lights . . . carol singers . . . presents for the children, of course. Perhaps she could even persuade Ran to don a red coat and white whiskers . . . Her eyes glinted for a moment, then, 'Well, I'll have to check with Ran, of course,' she said sedately, 'but I'm sure he'll be delighted.'

'And of course, dear, if you're—er—not feeling quite up to it by then,' Mrs Pearson said delicately, 'Mrs Bennett and I will be happy to organise it.' As Mellie stared at her blankly, she added meaningfully, 'Mr Owen won't want you worrying about it, I'm sure.'

Mellie gaped at her, the blinding light of comprehension blazing into her mind like a comet. She heard the echo of her mother's laugh. 'Mrs Pearson—she's incredible! Even worse than you, Livy. I'll swear she knows before the girl does.'

But was she—could she possibly be——? She caught the housekeeper's knowing look and said hastily, 'Thank you, Mrs Pearson. I'll give Mrs Bennett a ring later.'

Upstairs, she stared at herself in the mirror, her heart beating violently. Could it be true—that first disastrous night of the honeymoon? Surely not. And yet—she was three weeks overdue. But that was not unusual for her at times of stress and she had simply taken no account of it. True, she had felt very queasy the previous day, but that was only because she'd overslept, then dashed downstairs and forced herself to eat a breakfast she didn't want in her hurry to keep her nine o'clock appointment with the landscape architect. On a sudden impulse, she made up her mind to go into Shrewsbury today—now, instead of the next day, as she had previously intended.

All the rest of that day she was in a fever of

uncertainty, every slight twinge of her body, every barely perceptible stomach rumble seen suddenly in a possible new light. She set the alarm clock very early, but she was already wide awake before its shrill stridency made her jump. She opened a drawer, took out the small packet she had bought in the chemist's and went through to the bathroom . . .

An hour later, looking rather pale but somehow avoiding Mrs Pearson's penetrating eye, she went off to Ran's office in the main building. She worked as efficiently as she could all day, but her mind felt very remote from the room, from the desk she was mechanically toiling at.

Often, when she was alone, she spread her hands across her flat stomach and whispered, 'I'm having Ran's child,' and a little thrill of joy would bubble through her, but then, like a trickle of icy water, those other thoughts would invade her mind: Would Ran be glad? He was so jealous of her; would he be willing to share her, her body, with his baby, or would he regard the child as an interloper? And he himself had been so disregarded, neglected as a child; might the ability to want, never mind *love*, his own child have been all but destroyed?

Mellie finished work early, quite unable to concentrate any longer on the rows of figures in front of her, then spent the rest of the afternoon mooning around their part of the Manor, picking things up, setting them down, and finally staring out of the window at nothing.

At last she glanced at her watch. 'Oh, *no*, it was still only midday in New York and Ran would surely be out. He might have come back though, to prepare for

a business lunch . . . She found the number he had
left her and carefully dialled 010-1-212, then his
Manhattan hotel, but the desk clerk told her that
there was no reply from his room. Tears of vexation
sprang to her eyes and she began prowling around
the room again. Half an hour later she tried once
more, but he was still out.

Oh, this was ridiculous! She was being such a fool.
He would most probably ring her himself about
eleven, anyway, as he had done the previous two
evenings. She would go for a walk. She was just
going off downstairs when the phone rang. Ran—the
hotel had told him she'd called and he was ringing
her. She snatched up the receiver.

'Mellie, is that you?' The voice, a man's, was
somehow familiar, yet she couldn't place it.

She suppressed her disappointment. 'Yes.'

'It's Jason here.'

Just for a moment, after the joy and turbulence of
the day, her brain refused to function, and she
frowned in bewilderment. Who on earth was Jason?
Then, 'Jason?' she said warily.

'Yes. Look, Mellie, about—that night. Don't hang
up on me, please,' as a faint gasp of dismay escaped
her. 'You must let me apologise. It was unpardonable
of me—I was a drunken swine.'

'Oh, please don't,' she began awkwardly. He was
so obviously upset that she felt embarrassed for
him.

'At least say you forgive me.' He was pleading
now.

'Yes, of course I do, Jason. I've forgotten all about
it, honestly, and you really must do the same.'

He breathed a sigh of relief. 'Oh, you always were a sweetie, Mellie darling. Thank you. Now look,' his voice changed gear smoothly, 'I've been up in your neck of the woods filming a commercial. I'm staying at the Regent Arms, and you must let me buy you dinner this evening as a penance.'

'Oh, I couldn't possibly——'

'But I insist. Besides, you'll be doing a lonely man a good turn, my sweet. I'm stuck here for the evening, all on my own.'

'But you don't understand, Jason. It isn't that I don't want to——' though she didn't, not in the least '—but I'm married now. Married to Ran,' she added hesitantly.

'Yes, I did hear something to that effect. Congrats, darling, and I hope you'll both be very happy.' His voice rang with sincerity. 'Bring—your husband along too, why don't you?'

'He's away for a few days.'

'Well then, surely you won't begrudge me a couple of hours? Just come for a teeny drink, if you'd rather.'

Mellie laughed. Jason's charm was quite irresistible, and besides, the silent house was beginning to prey on her oppressively. She would just have to make sure that she was back well before Ran phoned. 'All right, I'll come.'

Dinner at the large, rather impersonal hotel was surprisingly good and throughout the meal Jason was at his amusing best, recounting one racy anecdote after another about the actors and actresses he had worked with until Mellie's sides ached with laughing. Finally, almost reluctantly, she reached for her bag.

'I must go, Jason. Thank you so much—it's been a lovely evening. I've really enjoyed it.'

With a spontaneous gesture, she held out her hand to him. To her surprise, a strange, enigmatic expression flickered momentarily in his eyes, but then he reached for her hand and bent to kiss it. 'My pleasure, darling.'

She smiled warmly at him, but as she stood up, a surge of dizziness suddenly swept through her and she clutched at the table.

'Are you all right, Mellie?'

'Oh, yes.' She shook her head to try to clear it. 'It must be that second glass of wine—I'm not really used to it.' Or, more likely, the baby, she thought. Just for a second, she thought of telling Jason her news, but no—she didn't want anyone to know until she'd told Ran.

Jason solicitously escorted her out to her car, and it was just as she was fishing in her bag for her keys that the dizziness struck again, only fifty times worse this time. She gave a gasp and her bag fell, unheeded, as she reeled against the car, feeling the metal cold against her clammy hands.

Jason, his face swollen to a huge size, seemed to advance, then retreat, then advance again in a strange, horrible dance. She put her hand out and tried to say, 'Please—help me,' but her tongue was glued to the roof of her mouth. She was dimly conscious that another shape—a man, but she could not recognise him—had appeared beside Jason. Strong hands were lifting her by the arms, she was being half dragged, half carried, her head lolling to one side, her feet scuffing the gravel, then without warning an intense, starless blackness descended on her, like everlasting night.

She was lying on a bed, in an unfamiliar room, and someone was bending over her. 'Ran?' she heard her own voice whisper, but then as she stared up through half-closed eyes, the figure resolved itself into Jason and recollection flooded back. She must have passed out in the car park. She'd just found her keys, when——

Weakly, she closed her eyes against the faint nausea which still flickered through her, then, as Jason hauled her upright, she slumped against him. He put a glass to her lips and she greedily drained the cold water.

'More?'

'N-no, thank you.' In spite of the water, her mouth was so furred that she could scarcely get the words out. 'I'm so sorry, Jason.' Embarrassment swept through her. 'I feel such a fool. I just don't know what came over me.'

It must have been the wine. She shouldn't have drunk anything, now she was—— Oh, heavens, the baby! Instinctively, one hand went to her stomach, palm pressed against it in a protective gesture.

'Feel better now?' There was an odd, half elated, nervous quality to Jason's normally assured voice. Well, she must have all but frightened him out of his wits.

'Y-yes, I do.' She gave him a weak, reassuring smile, then tentatively swung her legs over the edge of the bed and stood up. The room tilted crazily around her for a moment so that she had to stifle a gasp, but as she forced herself to stay upright it steadied.

'Are you quite sure you're all right?' Jason was still looking really concerned. 'Look, I haven't got my car with me, but let me ring for a taxi.'

'No—no.' She didn't want to wait any longer now. She had to get back home, before Ran phoned. 'If I could just have another drink of water.'

'Of course, Mellie.'

Jason hurried to the basin and filled another glass to overflowing for her, then guided her down the rear fire exit stairs to the car park. As she drove carefully away, he did not return her wave but stood watching her until she was out of sight. Her head was throbbing painfully, but fortunately there was no traffic on the road, except one police patrol car which cruised along unnervingly behind her for several miles before turning off towards the motorway.

The front door was unlocked; she let herself in and hauled herself wearily up the main staircase. The immense living-room was in darkness, with just one small pool of soft light where a table lamp was still burning. She moved towards it to switch it off, then stopped dead. At the extreme edge of the circle of lamplight a man was sitting in one of the armchairs, so still that she had almost missed seeing him.

She gave a little sob of joy. 'Oh, Ran, you're home! But how did you get back?'

'The usual way.'

He drained the glass of whisky he was holding and set it down, clinking against the bottle. 'Where have you been, Melissa?'

He had made no move to get up, and something in his stillness and the quietly spoken question froze her, even as she took an eager step towards him.

'I—I've been out for the evening.'

'For the evening? Until three in the morning?'

'Three in the——!' Instinctively, Mellie looked towards the carriage clock on the mantelshelf, and her eyes widened in horrified incredulity. 'But I don't understand——'

'Don't you?' It was a sneer. 'Surely you know how time flies when you're enjoying yourself?'

But she'd blacked out for only a few minutes, hadn't she? If it had been for any longer, surely Jason would have told her?

'I've only been away four days, Melissa. Couldn't you even wait that long? Did you have to go off, like a vixen on heat?'

A terrible fear was gripping her whole body, paralysing her mind so that she could not think.

'No, Ran, you don't understand. It wasn't how it looks. I—I've been out for a meal, and then, when I was leaving—before ten—I wanted to be here in case you rang.' A little sob all but choked her. 'I—it must have been the wine—I fainted.'

'Oh, yes—and you've been unconscious for the past five hours, I suppose.'

'Yes, I must have been. Look, ring Jason. He'll explain.'

'Jason!' Too late, as she saw the expression on his face, she realised the appalling blunder she'd made. 'You mean you've been with Jason Hancox?' He sprang from his chair now and crossed the room with the lethal speed of a panther, and she cowered away from the naked, uncontrollable rage flaring in his eyes. 'Hancox—of all men! How could you, you little——'

He seized her by the shoulders and shook her hard, so that her neck whiplashed back. Then, swinging her round, he thrust her in front of the gilt-framed mirror, his fingers digging cruelly into her soft skin so that she had to bite back a moan of pain.

'Look at yourself!'

Horrified, she saw her dress dishevelled, black curls tumbling in disorder across her brow, the dark shadows beneath her eyes, her lips swollen and pouting—for all the world as though she had indeed just returned from a night of illicit love.

'No, it's not true. However it looks, it's not true, Ran. You must believe me!'

'Believe you, you little tramp? Give me just one reason why I should.' His mouth tightened in an unyielding line of disgust. 'What a fool I was! I cut short my business in the States because I couldn't stay away from you a day longer, and then——'

'You must listen to me, Ran, before it's too late!' Mellie clutched convulsively at his arm, but he thrust her away.

'No, I won't listen to you. Maybe you were right that other night, after all. You did put a spell on me, you damned witch—but the spell's broken now!'

Their reflections stared wildly out at each other from the mirror, and at the sight of the raw fury in his face hot tears pricked at her eyes. But she would not cry in front of him. It was no use, she could see that, but some vestige of pride in herself made her speak.

'Yes, you're right. Whatever I say, you w-won't believe me. You've tried and condemned me already—you'd decided I was guilty even before I got back, so there's nothing more for me to say to you.'

For long moments they both stood motionless, then Ran suddenly pushed her away from him and strode across to the door. Mellie clasped her hands tightly in a vain attempt to still the dreadful shaking that was taking hold of her entire body.

'Where are you going?'

'To see Hancox—to finish the business that I should have settled that night. Where is he?'

'No, Ran, you mustn't!' Stark terror made her voice shrill. In this mood, Ran would surely kill Jason. Then, as he came menacingly back towards her, 'I shan't tell you.' She shook her head vehemently. 'Never.' He was right up to her now. 'No matter what you do to me, I shan't tell you. Not for his sake, I swear, but for yours.'

He stared down at her, then his face twisted and he turned on his heel. Minutes later, she heard his car roar into life and race off down the drive.

She waited until the sound was swallowed by the still night air, then, hugging herself as though she was cold, she backed up against the nearest wall. Her legs crumpled and she slid slowly down, until she was sitting propped up like a broken toy. From among all the chaos of her mind, one thought came suddenly to her: she hadn't told Ran about the baby.

The stiff lines of her face disintegrated as at last the bitter tears came.

CHAPTER TEN

MELLIE did not know what time it was when she finally aroused herself from her stupor of crying. She only knew that it was getting light, the first twitterings of the dawn chorus had begun—and Ran had not returned.

She dragged herself upstairs and collapsed on to the bed, willing herself to fall into a pit of oblivion, but instead she lay awake for hour after sleepless hour until, at last, she heard the front door open. She sprang up, then realised that the ponderous footsteps were those of Mrs Pearson. She couldn't see her—she couldn't see anyone, ever. Her whole being, flayed by Ran's cruelty, cringed at the mere thought of meeting sympathetic, never mind curious eyes.

She forced herself off the bed and went over to the dressing-table, but the reflection she saw shocked her brutally out of her apathy: her eyes dull and heavy, her pallid face ugly, blotched with tears. Oh, why hadn't he killed her and been done with it? He'd obviously wanted to—she'd seen it clearly in those hostile grey eyes.

But then her glance strayed downwards and she put a hand to her stomach in that protective gesture again, at the same time setting her soft lips in a line of steely determination. Somehow, for the sake of

Ran's—of *their* child, she would get through this waking nightmare. Her marriage was over, but out of its ashes this baby, who was so precious, would come to her.

She ran cold water into the basin and stooped to splash her face. Half an hour later, her features carefully obscured by several layers of make-up and wraparound sunglasses, she caught up her bag and went downstairs. She could hear Mrs Pearson in the kitchen as she fled out to the drive, where her car was still standing. So much had happened since she had got home that, like Rip Van Winkle, she could hardly come to terms with the mundane, everyday world that she had re-entered.

Ran's Jaguar was parked outside the main part of the Manor. He was back, then. Had he managed to track down Jason, and if he had——? Her mind shied away from the thought, but surely Jason would have booked out of the hotel and been safely out of harm's way long before now—temporarily, at least. Out of the corner of her eye, she saw someone—Ran?—in the entrance, but, not allowing herself a second look, she accelerated hard away.

With no clear idea of where she would go, she drove around for hours and finally found herself at the Long Mynd in the Shropshire Hills, one of the places she loved most. She parked in the towering shadow of Bodbury Ring, the huge Iron Age fortress, and sat staring across the tumbling stream at its precipitous sides, where a young couple were climbing, far up like a pair of insects.

Once, when she was fifteen, her parents safely out

of the way for the day, she had pestered Ran into bringing her here on his old motorbike. They too had climbed—or rather, he had pulled her up, protesting as the bracken and heather scratched her ankles, then they had collapsed in a laughing heap at the top. That had been the day that she had first realised what she had known subconsciously most of her conscious life: that she loved this wayward, moody lad. And it had been that day also that, without warning, she had caught an expression in his eyes and something had shimmered between them in the still, heather-scented air, a soft vibration, as though the strings of fate were pulling them, entwining them together . . .

She closed her eyes as she struggled to subdue the bitter gall that welled up inside her. What folly had brought her to this place today? And yet she was strangely reluctant to leave, so she made herself get out of the car and walk on up the valley.

Almost unaware of her surroundings, she wandered on, stumbling often on the uneven path. At the meeting of two cascading streams, she hesitated, then jumped across on the stepping-stones and climbed a little way up beside the right-hand one and sat in the shade of a stunted hawthorn tree, her head resting against its trunk. Below her, the way she had climbed, was a steep hillside of dark rock. Her father had once told her that this was some of the oldest rock in the whole world, almost as old as the earth itself, and she had paddled across the stream to put her hands on it in childish wonderment.

Now, as she idly leaned forward and dipped her hands into the fast-running water, its icy chill jerked

her back abruptly to the present, and blind panic
finally swept through her. What was she going to do?
But maybe, in the end, she wouldn't have to do
anything—Ran had taken over her life so completely
these last few months, he had probably already
determined what was going to happen. Perhaps he
would decide that he wasn't going to live with her
any longer . . . How could she bear that? Her fingers
clenched until the knuckles stood out white and
bony, and suddenly she thought, of course, if that
happened she wouldn't tell him about the baby—she
couldn't bear for him to keep her just for that, out of
pity or a grim sense of obligation.

As she looked across the stream again at the
ancient, primaeval rocks and the distant hills beyond,
there came into her mind lines that had been inspired
by that same Shropshire landscape:

For nature, heartless, witless nature,
Will neither care nor know
What stranger's feet may find the meadow
And trespass there and go,
Nor ask amid the dews of morning
If they are mine or no.

Housman's sad lines captured her own mood exactly,
but they brought her no solace. After all, it was with
very much the same thought that she had sought to
comfort herself when she looked out at those timeless
Lakeland fells on her honeymoon—on the very night,
in fact, in which their child had been conceived—and
that had been merely the prelude to the dreadful
half-life she had lived ever since, at least

until that wonderful, fleeting night when Ran had come to her in the maze.

But that was over now, destroyed by her own folly and Ran's unreasoning jealousy, and she knew with sudden clarity that she could not return to that other existence—not only for her own sake but for their baby's as well, for the child would soon enough understand that it had been born into a house totally bereft of love. No—she would face Ran again, brave his fierce anger once more, if needs be, but she had to make one last attempt, which would either save them or destroy their marriage forever.

It was late afternoon when she got back. As she parked her car, her resolution faltered for a moment, but then she mounted the main staircase, clutching the carved banister for support, and went into the living-room. Then she stopped dead as, at exactly the same moment, Ran entered the room from the spiral stairway.

He too halted abruptly when he saw her and they stared at one another across the expanse of room. His face was almost colourless; his mouth was drawn down into a thin, pale line, and there were surely lines on his brow that had not been there before. She ached to run to him, hold him in her arms and soothe away those marks of strain, but pride—and the certainty that he would curtly rebuff her, or worse, if she did held her motionless.

'Oh, Mrs Owen.' She almost leapt out of her skin as from below she heard the housekeeper's voice, shattering the tension into fragments, 'Is your husband there?'

'Yes, Mrs Pearson, he's here.' Mellie spoke without looking round, keeping her eyes fixed on Ran, then finally turned as, behind her, Mrs Pearson reached the top stair.

'Would you give him this, please? I found it in the hall. It must have come by special messenger, but no one saw it delivered.'

She handed Mellie a large brown foolscap envelope, then caught sight of Ran. She opened her mouth to speak, then obviously thought better of it and retreated again as Mellie stared blankly down at the typewritten address label: 'Ranulf Owen. Private and Confidential'.

'I'll have that.'

She was not aware that Ran had moved until his hand came up to take the envelope from her. Without a word, she passed it to him and he turned away. She was crossing the room towards the spiral staircase, but spun round as she heard him swear savagely. The envelope had dropped unheeded to the floor and he was staring down at something—a sheaf of what looked like photographs—in his hand, an expression of sick disgust on his face. A terrible premonition of evil was sweeping through her.

'What is it? What's wrong?' she faltered.

By way of reply, he threw the photographs down on to the coffee table so that they skewed across it and several slithered on to the floor, then went and stood, staring out of the window.

Somehow, Mellie walked across to the table, putting each foot carefully down in front of her as though she was teetering on the treacherous crust of a swamp which might give way and suck her down. She stooped beside the table, clumsily gathering them up, then as she saw the top photograph she became very still. She stared down at it, then dropped it as if its touch contaminated her, glanced at the next, and the next, then flung the rest down, her hands trembling.

'Next time you go off to meet your lover,' his voice was almost, but not quite, controlled, 'you really ought to make sure that you haven't got a photographer in tow.'

'It isn't true—it can't be true!' She caught sight of one of the photographs again and clutched her hand to her mouth to force down the spasm of retching nausea.

'You'll have to do better than that, *darling*.' The contempt in his voice seared her. 'After all, you know what they say—the camera never lies.'

'But I told you—I had a blackout. Jason——' she stopped, staring down at the man in the pictures. The photographer had obviously been at great pains to capture as much of her face and naked body as possible; the man had been relatively unimportant, but he was clearly recognisable, nonetheless, and her heart constricted with the pain of Jason's betrayal.

She swallowed. 'You must believe me. I didn't do anything wrong—at least, not knowingly. Jason must have fixed this up.' Fighting back her aversion, she made herself study the photographs more closely. 'If you look, my eyes are closed in all the——'

'Ecstasy?'

The ice-cold tone made her shiver. She stared up at that inexorable back, then very slowly got to her feet. She was already turning away, when something almost outside herself halted her. Whatever the cost, she had to try once more.

'I swear to you, Ran,' her voice was almost inaudible, 'whatever these horrible photographs may seem to show, they are a lie. You must believe me.'

At last, he turned slowly back to her and stood leaning against the window-frame. 'I only wish I could!'

'No, you don't, not really.' Mellie spoke with sudden insight. 'You want me to be guilty—it feeds your crazy jealousy. I told you—in the m-maze,' she faltered into silence under the sheer pain of those sweet, remembered images, then went on even more quietly, 'I've never in my life looked at another man, much less loved one, but you prefer not to believe that. You're still punishing me for something I did when I was sixteen.'

She paused to allow him to speak, but when he only stared at her, frowning slightly as though he hardly saw her, she gave him a small, sad smile. 'I told you last night——' No, that was wrong. She pressed her fingers to her throbbing temple. Had it really been earlier that day? '—this morning, nothing I say will make any difference. I love you, but you'll never trust me, and without trust there's nothing——'

The phone shrilled, making them both start

violently. Ran muttered something under his breath, then strode across to his desk and snatched up the receiver.

'Owen here,' he snapped, but then Mellie, watching him lethargically, saw him stiffen. 'Yes, I have seen them.' She took a tentative step towards him, then stopped as she saw the expression on his face. 'Well, well, I might have known who was behind this filth!'

Mellie clutched at her throat. Ran seemed almost to have forgotten her presence, but when she made another move towards him he waved her away peremptorily. As she stood still, rooted to the spot, he clapped his hand over the receiver and said harshly, 'Get out!'

Quailing before the fury in his eyes, she retreated, but once outside the door, her weariness forgotten, she raced upstairs to the bedroom, paused for a moment to gather her breath, then stealthily lifted the extension receiver.

'. . . make interesting viewing, don't you agree?' The tone was measured, silky, the voice of a man totally in control of the situation, she thought suddenly, with sick apprehension.

'I rather guessed that Hancox was just a tool in someone else's hands.' Ran's clipped voice was scarcely recognisable.

The man's laugh jarred against Mellie's ear. 'Yes, but a very willing tool. I'm afraid you've got a bad enemy there, Owen. It appears that you made rather a mess of those boyish good looks—lost him a part he was very keen on. In any case,' that sneering laugh again, 'he quite fancies that trusting little wife of yours. He was sorry that it was all make-believe, just for the benefit of the camera. Mind you, he wasn't all that happy about doping her, but an extra thousand overcame his delicate scruples.'

Unseen, Mellie closed her eyes against the joy and relief that, above all the other tumultuous emotions, were threatening to overwhelm her. At least Ran now knew the truth of her innocence!

'Of course, he thought it was just a way of getting back at you—he'd no idea what I really intended.'

'And what precisely do you intend?' Still that alien voice.

'You've been queering my pitch for just too long, Owen—ever since Ginny,' Mellie's knuckles whitened on the receiver, 'that oh, so charming ex-wife of mine opened her——' she winced at the crude expletive '—mouth of hers once too often.'

'What was that to you? You know very well I wasn't exactly the first—or the last—of your employees to enjoy her favours.'

'No, but you were the only one not content to leave it there, weren't you? I didn't give a damn about what she got up to in bed, but nobody—least of all a penniless upstart like you—beats me in the market-place and gets away with it.'

'Yes, that's just where your priorities would lie, of course.'

'Too right they do. Now listen, Owen,' Mellie could sense the long-held malice breaking through the man's voice, 'about this deal you're working on in the States——'

'Oh, so you know about that?'

'Of course. That's the only way I could persuade Hancox to take on the job, knowing that you were safely out of the country. Anyway, that particular deal isn't going through.'

'You think not?'

'No.'

Silence hung between the two men and Mellie almost stopped breathing. They were like two duellists, she thought involuntarily—old enemies who knew well the other's strengths and weaknesses, and this time Ran was fighting with one arm tied behind his back.

'You see, if it does,' that hateful voice again, 'your wife's lovely body will be displayed on every bookstall in the country. I'm sure you wouldn't want every lascivious male in the——'

'You wouldn't dare!'

'Try me.'

'There's such a thing as the Obscene Publications Act, you know. Not even the gutter Press would dare handle them.'

'Oh, some minor adjustments will put them on the right side of the law. But in any case, it's not the tabloids I have in mind. Are you forgetting that—er—fine art magazine I own?' His voice hardened. 'Those pictures will be in the next edition, unless I receive by tomorrow an assurance in writing that you're withdrawing from the deal.'

'All right.' Ran's voice was completely devoid of emotion. 'You'll get it in the morning——'

Afterwards, Mellie was never quite sure how she'd

got down the stairs. As she almost tumbled into the room, Ran was saying, '. . . trust you to send me the negatives?' She snatched the phone from him.

'Don't hang up just yet.' She was fighting to get her breath, but as Ran made a grab for the receiver she fiercely swept his hand aside. 'This is Melissa Owen here.'

'Good afternoon, Mrs Owen.' If he was disconcerted, he was not showing it. 'I don't think we've——'

'I've heard what you've been saying to my husband——'

'Now, this has nothing to do with you, my dear. This is entirely between me and your husband.'

'Are you forgetting what's in those photographs?' she snapped. 'But in any case, if it concerns my husband, it concerns me. And I'm sure you'll be aware that, as I'm his newly appointed business partner, he needs my signature for any transaction,' she did not dare look at Ran as the lie flowed fluently from her lips, 'and I'm telling you now that I'll walk through fire before I give it to him for this!'

'But Mrs Owen,' the smooth mask was beginning to slip, 'I don't think you quite realise what the unfortunate consequences of that will be.'

'I realise perfectly well. You can go ahead and publish those pictures in your filthy magazine. Everyone who knows me—who cares for me,' Mellie glanced at Ran, but he was sitting with his head bent, doodling on a scrap of paper, 'will know that I'm totally innocent, and for the rest—well, they can think what they like.'

'Don't try to fool with me, Mrs Owen. Your husband is too proud a man ever to allow it.' Did she detect behind the bluster the faintest hint of uncertainty? In any case, her anger was now buoying her up, sweeping her along.

'On this occasion, he'll have no choice in the matter. But let me just tell you this—if you do go ahead, I promise you I shall be at our solicitor's office first thing tomorrow morning. I shall make a sworn affidavit and then we shall go to the police.' She paused for maximum effect. 'Blackmail. I don't think your shareholders will take very kindly to that, do you? Think it over very carefully, but don't take too long. Those negatives, and any other prints, will be in our hands by tomorrow morning, or——'

She left the threat unfinished, hoping desperately that she had infused sufficient menace and conviction into her voice. A vicious obscenity came hurtling down the line, then it went dead.

Her hands were shaking uncontrollably and the receiver clattered as she set it down. She looked at Ran, but he was still sitting, head lowered.

'Will he still go ahead, do you think?' she asked.

'Oh, no. I'm sure not. You called his bluff completely.'

'But Jason—surely publicity like that would have done him no good at all?'

Ran laughed shortly. 'Friend Jason had got way out of his depth. He'll have just thought he was driving a wedge between us—not going public. So he ought to be grateful to you too.' There was a long silence. Mellie was willing him to look up at her, but he only said, his voice still unnaturally terse, 'I had no idea that US deal meant so much to you.'

'Oh, damn your stupid business deal, whatever it is!' she burst out. 'Do you think I care that much——' she snapped her fingers contemptuously '—for it? Whatever I did, it was because I love you, and for no other reason. Oh, yes,' she broke off, then went on, a trace of bitterness in her voice, 'one other reason. This time, I wanted to show you that I've grown up, that I can stand up for you. You thought I never could, and I wanted to prove you wrong. But of course you won't believe that.'

All the euphoria of her triumph had evaporated and she turned away, weary, but Ran caught at her hand, gently but inexorably pulling her back.

'Mellie, I'm sorry.' His voice was unsteady, and when their eyes at last met, incredibly, she saw the sheen of tears in his.

'Oh, no, Ran, please—don't!' She gathered him to her, cradling his head against her breast, burying her lips in his thick hair. 'It's all right, it's all right,' she said over and over again, until at last she felt the tension drain from his rigid body.

He pulled away from her slightly and looked up at her. 'Forgive me, my darling—if you can.'

All the defences of this proud, hard man were down and she held him totally in her power. She could so easily exact a terrible revenge—for his jealousy, his cruelty, for all the anguish he had cost her . . .

She gently brushed his lips with her finger. 'For what?'

'For having almost wantonly tried to destroy the only thing that's more precious to me than life itself—your love,' he said slowly, then went on, 'It isn't too late, is it?'

She shook her head and smiled, hardly able to see him through the blur of her own happy tears. 'No, Ran, it's not too late,' and he stood up and gathered her into the protective circle of his arms, her head against his chest, his cheek against her soft hair.

She lost all count of how long they stood there, their arms round each other, utterly at peace. When the phone shrilled again they both tensed warily, then Mellie made herself snatch it up. She listened for a moment, then said, 'Thank you, yes. I'll ask him now.'

When Ran looked enquiringly at her, she said, 'It's Mrs Bennett. She wants to know if we'll host the party for the Sunday School children here next Christmas.'

Ran took the phone. 'Hello, Mrs Bennett. Yes, of course, by all means. There's just one problem, though. Melissa and I won't be here this Christmas, but you're more than welcome to go ahead and use the Manor without us.'

'Won't be here?' faltered Mellie as he replaced the receiver. Weren't they going to spend their first Christmas at home? 'But why ever not?' she wailed.

Ran silenced her with a kiss. 'Because, my sweet Lissy, I'm taking you away then, for that honeymoon

in the sun I deprived you of.' He slanted her a
wicked grin. 'It's really disturbed my sleep at nights,
the thought of all those gorgeous bikinis lying unused, so—it's Christmas in the Seychelles for
us.'

'The Seychelles?' she repeated slowly, then went
on, not quite looking at him. 'If you wouldn't mind
too much, Ran, the first trip we have abroad, can it be
to Portugal, the Algarve?'

She sensed him stiffen momentarily, then,
'Whatever you want, my darling.' She turned to him
now and he gave her a rueful grin. 'I suppose I can
always let him beat me at golf a few times. Would
that transform me into the ideal son-in-law, do you
think?'

This was the moment. Mellie paused, then, her
heart doing an unsteady pit-pat, she said very softly,
'Oh, I can think of something much better than that.
Like telling him about his first grandchild.'

For a long moment, comprehension did not dawn,
but then, as she looked up at him, hardly breathing,

'You mean——?' She nodded, and blank shock,
astonishment, fleetingly something very akin to
panic chased across his face, then finally, 'Oh, my
sweet love!'

He gripped her in a convulsive bear-hug, then, as
she gave a little breathless squeak, just as hastily
released her. 'I'm sorry, I suppose I shouldn't—not
now.' He smiled down at her, the tenderness welling
in his eyes. 'I was just thinking—a little girl, with

black curls and green eyes.'

'Oh, no,' she said dreamily, shaking her head against his chest, 'I've got a feeling this one's a boy. Next time, perhaps . . .'

'And you don't mind, do you?' Ran tilted her face, searching it anxiously.

'I wish maybe we'd got just a little more time on our own, but,' she pretended to ponder the question, 'as you're so obviously intent on firmly establishing the Owen dynasty, like some twentieth-century Border baron, I think the sooner I make a start, the better.'

'Hmm, I suppose you think that, as my new, self-appointed business partner,' he grinned at her, 'you can get away with remarks like that. But anyway, if we can't go away at Christmas, we'll go now—tomorrow.'

'But the first guests are due in less than a month!'

'Oh, damn the guests. Anyway, we'll be back long before then, and the staff can carry on getting organised perfectly well without us. In any case,' he grimaced, 'I rather think there'll be rejoicing all round if I disappear for a couple of weeks. This last month or so, I've hardly been their idea of an ideal employer.'

'Oh, are you ever?' Mellie asked demurely, then went on hastily, 'But please, Ran, I don't want to go to the Seychelles—not this time, anyway. There's this place I know, it would be marvellous for a honeymoon—just a lake, and mountains, and solitude.'

CHAPTER ELEVEN

FROM behind the blackness of the mountain, the rim of the sun appeared quite suddenly, turning the dark expanse of lake to metallic silver. Mellie pulled up the sheet around them, then leaned back comfortably against Ran's chest. His arms around her, they watched as the sun slid clear of the last ridge, turning the sky to lemon, then palest apricot. It was going to be another lovely day.

She sighed in contentment, and Ran asked softly, 'Happy, love?'

'Mmm. I just wish we could stay here forever.'

'So do I. But——'

'I know,' she laughed. 'The kitchen staff are starting on Monday, and——'

'No, it's not that. But you see, I've had to put Jackie off once. It wouldn't be fair——'

'Jackie?' Mellie wasn't aware how much she had tensed, until she heard the sudden note of strain in her voice. Jackie—the unknown owner of that beautiful earring? One of Ran's—— Oh, how could he?

'Yes, my secretary from way back. She was like a mother hen to me when I first started and I've always been very fond of her.' He paused, but when she didn't speak, went on, 'She and David have been up

185

here for holidays a couple of times since I bought the place, and she had asked me if they could borrow it for their twentieth wedding anniversary. But of course, as we were coming, I had to put them off.'

'You——' Mellie began.

'Yes?' Ran's tone was all polite enquiry.

'Last time—you let me think——'

'Jealous, were you?' He was grinning down at her in unconcealed triumph. 'But you really can't blame me if you leapt to the wrong conclusion.'

'Oh you—you!' and she beat her small fists against his bare chest until he captured both her wrists in one hand and pushed her back against the pillow. 'Now, don't you dare move. I'll go and get breakfast while you decide what you'd like to do today.' And when she gave him a deliberately provocative smile, 'Apart from that, I mean.'

'I told you last night, I want to climb that mountain—Haystacks.'

Ran scowled at her. 'And I told *you*, you're not climbing any mountains. We'll drive to Buttermere, if you like—have a little walk round the lake,' cajolingly, 'and then we'll have lunch at the Fish Inn.'

Mellie sat bolt upright in the bed, more than matching his scowl. 'Now look here, you know what the doctor said. I'm absolutely fine and——'

'I know, I know. I'm to resist all temptation to treat you like a piece of precious crystal. It's all right for Bob Morgan,' grumbled Ran. 'He's a doctor, not a neurotic first-time father.'

'But you know very well that guide book said that grannies in high heels and babes in arms can go up Haystacks,' she said mutinously.

'Yes, but not babies in the womb.' But Ran eyed her thoughtfully, as though weighing her up, then gracefully conceded defeat. 'Well, if you promise to tell me the moment you get tired.'

'I promise,' she said meekly.

'Right, breakfast.' But when he briskly pushed the sheet aside she took hold of his arm.

'Not just yet,' she murmured, and traced her finger in light spirals down his bare chest, until she felt the faint tremor run through her body.

'You're not, by any chance, thinking of putting another spell on me?' he whispered against her mouth. 'Because if so, I have to tell you that this morning I feel totally impervious to any of your magic.'

Mellie moved her hand to rest it, fingers splayed, against his stomach. 'Oh, really? We'll just have to see about that, won't we?'

And moments later he surrendered with a groan, gathering her into his arms. 'Come here then, my provocative little green-eyed witch!'

HARLEQUIN
Romance®

Coming Next Month

#3079 THE ENDS OF THE EARTH Bethany Campbell
Jennifer Martinson wasn't just a "California sun bunny lost in the snow." But to Hal
Bailey, Arctic research scientist and avowed Martinson-hater, she was as out of place as
the two California gray whales he wished had stayed home, too.

#3080 UNLIKELY PLACES Anne Marie Duquette
On her Colorado vacation, Felicity Barrett walks into a job as a film extra, stumbles into
unexpected adventures—and falls into the arms of Seth Tyler. But Felicity fears that
Seth's ties to his hometown are stronger than their newfound love....

#3081 CONSOLATION PRIZE Catherine George
It might not be the best way to get acquainted with an attractive man—though Rhodri
apparently isn't put off when Hilary knocks him out, thinking he's an intruder. Hilary,
however, can't believe he's interested in her and not her glamorous sister.

#3082 AMBER AND AMETHYST Kay Gregory
Amber's father hopes her summer job at the Amethyst mine will keep her away from
unsuitable men. Instead, it leads her straight into the arms of Kyle Maki, an ex-university
professor turned bus driver. Kyle, scornful of her life-style and immaturity, thinks *she* is
unsuitable!

#3083 CARVILLE'S CASTLE Miriam MacGregor
Lucas Carville offered Sylvia his hand and his heart seven years ago, and she had laughed.
Unexpectedly, they meet again and she realizes all too clearly what a fool she'd been to
turn him down....

#3084 THE CONVENIENT WIFE Betty Neels
Most girls dream of a love match, but it seems an unlikely prospect for Venetia. Probably
that's why she accepts Duert ter Laan-Luitinga's offer of a marriage of convenience. The
only problem is she soons longs for a less cold-blooded arrangement.

**Available in October wherever paperback books are sold, or through
Harlequin Reader Service:**

In the U.S.
901 Fuhrmann Blvd.
P.O. Box 1397
Buffalo, N.Y. 14240-1397

In Canada
P.O. Box 603
Fort Erie, Ontario
L2A 5X3